PENGUIN BOOKS

FIREWORKS

Angela Carter was born in 1940. When she published her first novel, *Shadow Dance*, in 1965, she was immediately recognized as one of Britain's most original writers. Eight other novels followed: *The Magic Toyshop* (1967, John Llewellyn Rhys Prize), *Several Perceptions* (1968, Somerset Maugham Award), *Heroes and Villains* (1969), *Love* (1971), *The Infernal Desire Machines of Doctor Hoffman* (1972), *The Passion of New Eve* (1977), *Nights at the Circus* (1984, James Tait Black Memorial Prize), and *Wise Children* (1991). Angela Carter also published three collections of short stories—*The Bloody Chamber* (1979, Cheltenham Festival of Literature Award), *Fireworks: Nine Profane Pieces* (1984), and *Saints and Strangers* (1985, published in the UK as *Black Venus*)—two works of nonfiction, and a volume of radio plays. She translated the fairy stories of Charles Perrault and edited collections of fairy and folk tales as well as *Wayward Girls & Wicked Women: An Anthology of Subversive Stories* (1986). She also wrote the screenplay for the 1984 film *The Company of Wolves*, based on her short story.

From 1976 through 1978 Angela Carter was Arts Council of Great Britain Fellow in Creative Writing at Sheffield University, and from 1980 through 1981 she was visiting professor in the Writing Program at Brown University. She traveled and taught widely in the U.S. and Australia but lived in London. Angela Carter died in February, 1992.

FIREWORKS
Nine Profane Pieces

Angela Carter

PENGUIN BOOKS

PENGUIN BOOKS
Published by the Penguin Group
Penguin Books USA Inc.,
375 Hudson Street, New York, New York 10014, U.S.A.
Penguin Books Ltd, 27 Wrights Lane, London W8 5TZ, England
Penguin Books Australia Ltd, Ringwood,
Victoria, Australia
Penguin Books Canada Ltd, 10 Alcorn Avenue,
Toronto, Ontario, Canada M4V 3B2
Penguin Books (N.Z.) Ltd, 182–190 Wairau Road,
Auckland 10, New Zealand

Penguin Books Ltd, Registered Offices:
Harmondsworth, Middlesex, England

First published in Great Britain by Quartet Books Limited 1974
First published in the United States of America by Harper & Row 1981
Published in Penguin Books 1987

3 5 7 9 10 8 6 4 2

LIBRARY OF CONGRESS CATALOGING IN PUBLICATION DATA
Carter, Angela, 1940–
Fireworks: nine profane pieces.
Contents: A souvenir of Japan—The executioner's
beautiful daughter—The loves of lady purple—[etc.]
I. Title.
PR6053.A73F5 1987   823'.914   87-12119
ISBN 0 14 01.0588 3

Printed in the United States of America
Set in Baskerville

Contents

FIREWORKS

A Souvenir of Japan

WHEN I WENT OUTSIDE to see if he was coming home, some children dressed ready for bed in cotton nightgowns were playing with sparklers in the vacant lot on the corner. When the sparks fell down in beards of stars, the smiling children cooed softly. Their pleasure was very pure because it was so restrained. An old woman said: "And so they pestered their father until he bought them fireworks." In their language, fireworks are called *hannabi*, which means "flower fire." All through summer, every evening, you can see all kinds of fireworks, from the humblest to the most elaborate, and once we rode the train out of Shinjuku for an hour to watch one of the public displays which are held over rivers so that the dark water multiplies the reflections.

By the time we arrived at our destination, night had

already fallen. We were in the suburbs. Many families were on their way to enjoy the fireworks. Their mothers had scrubbed and dressed up the smallest children to celebrate the treat. The little girls were especially immaculate in pink and white cotton kimonos tied with fluffy sashes like swatches of candy floss. Their hair had been most beautifully brushed, arranged in sleek, twin bunches and decorated with twists of gold and silver thread. These children were all on their best behavior, because they were staying up late, and held their parents' hands with a charming propriety. We followed the family parties until we came to some fields by the river and saw, high in the air, fireworks already opening out like variegated parasols. They were visible from far away and, as we took the path that led through the fields towards their source, they seemed to occupy more and more of the sky.

Along the path were stalls where shirtless cooks with sweatbands round their heads roasted corncobs and cuttlefish over charcoal. We bought cuttlefish on skewers and ate them as we walked along. They had been basted with soy sauce and were very good. There were also stalls selling goldfish in plastic bags and others for big balloons with rabbit ears. It was like a fairground—but such a well-ordered fair! Even the patrolling policemen carried colored paper lanterns instead of torches. Everything was altogether quietly festive. Ice-cream sellers wandered among the crowd, ringing handbells. Their boxes of wares smoked with cold and they called out in plaintive voices, "Icy, icy, icy cream!" When young lovers dispersed discreetly down the tracks in the sedge, the shadowy, indefatigable salesmen pursued them with bells, lamps and mournful cries.

By now, a great many people were walking towards the

fireworks but their steps fell so softly and they chatted in such gentle voices there was no more noise than a warm, continual, murmurous humming, the cozy sound of shared happiness, and the night filled with a muted, bourgeois yet authentic magic. Above our heads, the fireworks hung dissolving earrings on the night. Soon we lay down in a stubbled field to watch the fireworks. But, as I expected, he very quickly grew restive.

"Are you happy?" he asked. "Are you sure you're happy?" I was watching the fireworks and did not reply at first although I knew how bored he was and, if he was himself enjoying anything, it was only the idea of my pleasure—or, rather, the idea that he enjoyed my pleasure, since this would be a proof of love. I became guilty and suggested we return to the heart of the city. We fought a silent battle of self-abnegation and I won it, for I had the stronger character. Yet the last thing in the world that I wanted was to leave the scintillating river and the gentle crowd. But I knew his real desire was to return and so return we did, although I do not know if it was worth my small victory of selflessness to bear his remorse at cutting short my pleasure, even if to engineer this remorse had, at some subterranean level, been the whole object of the outing.

Nevertheless, as the slow train nosed back into the thickets of neon, his natural liveliness returned. He could not lose his old habit of walking through the streets with a sense of expectation, as if a fateful encounter might be just around the corner, for, the longer one stayed out, the longer something remarkable might happen and, even if nothing ever did, the chance of it appeased the sweet ache of his boredom for a little while. Besides, his duty by me was done. He had taken me out for the evening and now he wanted to be rid of me. Or so I saw it. The word for wife, *okusan*, means the person who occupies the inner room and rarely, if ever, comes out of it. Since I often appeared to be his wife, I was frequently subjected to this treatment, though I fought against it bitterly.

But I usually found myself waiting for him to come home knowing, with a certain resentment, that he would not; and that he would not even telephone me to tell me he would be late, either, for he was far too guilty to do so. I had nothing better to do than to watch the neighborhood children light their sparklers and giggle; the old woman stood beside me and I knew she disapproved of me. The entire street politely disapproved of me. Perhaps they thought I was contributing to the delinquency of a juvenile for he was obviously younger than I. The old woman's back was bowed almost to a circle from carrying, when he was a baby, the father who now supervised the domestic fireworks in his evening *déshabillé* of loose, white, crepe drawers, naked to the waist. Her face had the seamed reserve of the old in this country. It was a neighborhood poignantly rich in old ladies.

At the corner shop, they put an old lady outside on an upturned beer crate each morning, to air. I think she must have been the household grandmother. She was so old she had lapsed almost entirely into a somnolent plant life. She was of neither more nor less significance to herself or to the world than the pot of morning glories which blossomed beside her and perhaps she had less significance than the flowers, which would fade before lunch was ready. They kept her very clean. They covered her pale cotton kimono with a spotless pinafore trimmed with coarse lace and she never dirtied it because she did not move. Now and then, a child came out to comb her hair. Her consciousness was quite beclouded by time and, when I passed by, her rheumy eyes settled upon me always with the same, vague, disinterested wonder, like that of an Eskimo watching a train. When she whispered, *Irrasyaimase,* the shopkeeper's word of welcome, in the ghostliest of whispers, like the rustle of a paper bag, I saw her teeth were rimmed with gold.

The children lit sparklers under a mouse-colored sky and, because of the pollution in the atmosphere, the moon was mauve. The cicadas throbbed and shrieked in the backyards. When I think of this city, I shall always remember the cicadas who whirr relentlessly all through the summer nights, rising to a piercing crescendo in the subfusc dawn. I have heard cicadas even in the busiest streets, though they thrive best in the back alleys, where they ceaselessly emit that scarcely tolerable susurration which is like a shrill intensification of extreme heat.

A year before, on such a throbbing, voluptuous, platitudinous, subtropical night, we had been walking down one of these shady streets together, in and out of the shadows of the willow trees, looking for somewhere to make love. Morning glories climbed the lattices which screened the low, wooden houses, but the darkness hid the tender colors of these flowers, which the Japanese prize because they fade so quickly. He soon found a hotel, for the city is hospitable to lovers. We were shown into a room like a paper box. It contained nothing but a mattress spread on the floor. We lay down immediately and began to kiss one another. Then a maid soundlessly opened the sliding door and, stepping out of her slippers, crept in on stockinged feet, breathing apologies. She carried a tray which contained two cups of tea and a plate of candies. She put the tray down on the matted floor beside us and backed, bowing and apologizing, from the room while our uninterrupted kiss continued. He started to unfasten my shirt and then she came back again. This time, she carried an armful of towels. I was stripped stark naked when she returned for a third time to bring the receipt for his money. She was clearly a most respectable woman and, if she was embarrassed, she did not show it by a single word or gesture.

I learned his name was Taro. In a toy store, I saw one of those books for children with pictures which are cunningly made of paper cut-outs so that, when you turn the page, the picture springs up in the three stylized dimensions of a backdrop in Kabuki. It was the story of Momotaro, who was born from a peach. Before my eyes, the paper peach split open and there was the baby, where the stone should have been. He, too, had the inhuman sweetness of a child born from something other than a mother, a passive, cruel sweetness I did not immediately understand, for it was that of the repressed masochism which, in my country, is usually confined to women.

Sometimes he seemed to possess a curiously unearthly quality when he perched upon the mattress with his knees drawn up beneath his chin in the attitude of a pixie on a doorknocker. At these times, his face seemed somehow both too flat and too large for his elegant body which had such curious, androgynous grace with its svelte, elongated spine, wide shoulders and unusually well developed pectorals, almost like the breasts of a girl approaching puberty. There was a subtle lack of alignment between face and body and he seemed almost goblin, as if he might have borrowed another person's head, as Japanese goblins do, in order to perform some devious trick. These impressions of a weird visitor were fleeting yet haunting. Sometimes, it was possible for me to believe he had practiced an enchantment upon me, as foxes in this country may, for, here, a fox can masquerade as human and at the best of times the high cheekbones gave to his face the aspect of a mask.

His hair was so heavy his neck drooped under its weight and was of a black so deep it turned purple in sunlight. His mouth also was purplish and his blunt, bee-stung lips those of Gauguin's Tahitians. The touch of his skin was as smooth as water as it flows through the fingers. His eyelids were retractable, like those of a cat, and sometimes disappeared completely. I should have liked to have had him embalmed and been able to keep him beside me in a glass coffin, so that I could watch him all the time and he would not have been able to get away from me.

As they say, Japan is a man's country. When I first came to Tokyo, cloth carps fluttered from poles in the gardens of the families fortunate enough to have borne boy children, for it was the time of the annual festival, Boys Day. At least they do not disguise the situation. At least one knows where one is. Our polarity was publicly acknowledged and socially sanctioned. As an example of the use of the word *dewa*, which occasionally means, as far as I can gather, "in," I once found in a textbook a sentence which, when translated, read: "In a society where men dominate, they value women only as the object of men's passions." If the only conjunction possible to us was that of the death-defying double-somersault of love, it is, perhaps, a better thing to be valued only as an object of passion than never to be valued at all. I had never been so absolutely the mysterious other. I had become a kind of phoenix, a fabulous beast; I was an outlandish jewel. He found me, I think, inexpressibly exotic. But I often felt like a female impersonator in Japan.

In the department store there was a rack of dresses labeled: "For Young and Cute Girls Only." When I looked at them, I felt as gross as Glumdalclitch. I wore men's sandals because they were the only kind that fitted me and, even so, I had to take the largest size. My pink cheeks, blue eyes and blatant yellow hair made of me, in the visual orchestration of this city in which all heads were dark, eyes brown and skin monotone, an instrument which played upon an alien scale. In a sober harmony of subtle plucked instruments and wistful flutes, I blared. I proclaimed myself like in a perpetual fanfare. He was so delicately put together that I thought his skeleton must have the airy elegance of a bird's and I was sometimes afraid that I might smash him. He told me that when he was in bed with me, he felt like a small boat upon a wide, stormy sea.

We pitched our tent in the most unlikely surroundings. We were living in a room furnished only by passion amongst homes of the most astounding respectability. The sounds around us were the swish of brooms upon *tatami* matting and the clatter of demotic Japanese. On all the window ledges, prim flowers bloomed in pots. Every morning, the washing came out on the balconies at seven. Early one morning, I saw a man washing the leaves of his tree. Quilts and mattresses went out to air at eight. The sunlight lay thick enough on these unpaved alleys to lay the dust and somebody always seemed to be practicing Chopin in one or another of the flimsy houses, so lightly glued together from plywood it seemed they were sustained only by willpower. Once I was at home, however, it was as if I occupied the inner room and he did not expect me to go out of it, although it was I who paid the rent.

Yet, when he was away from me, he spent much of the time savoring the most annihilating remorse. But this remorse or regret was the stuff of life to him and out he would go again the next night, or, if I had been particularly angry, he would wait until the night after that. And, even if he fully intended to come back early and had promised me he would do so, circumstances always somehow denied him and once more he would contrive to miss the last train. He and his friends spent their nights in a desultory progression from coffee shop to bar to *pachinko* parlor to coffee shop again, with the radiant aimlessness of the pure existential hero. They were connoisseurs of boredom. They savored the various bouquets of the subtly differentiated boredoms which rose from the long, wasted hours at the dead end of night. When it was time for the first train in the morning, he would go back to the mysteriously deserted, Piranesi perspectives of the station, discolored by dawn, exquisitely tortured by the notion—which probably contained within it a damped-down spark of hope—that, this time, he might have done something irreparable.

I speak as if he had no secrets from me. Well, then, you must realize that I was suffering from love and I knew him as intimately as I knew my own image in a mirror. In other words, I knew him only in relation to myself. Yet, on those terms, I knew him perfectly. At times, I thought I was inventing him as I went along, however, so you will have to take my word for it that we existed.

But I do not want to paint our circumstantial portraits so that we both emerge with enough well-rounded, spuriously detailed actuality that you are forced to believe in us. I do not want to practice such sleight of hand. You must be content only with glimpses of our outlines, as if you had caught sight of our reflections in the looking-glass of somebody else's house as you passed by the window. His name was not Taro. I only called him Taro so that I could use the conceit of the peach boy, because it seemed appropriate.

Speaking of mirrors, the Japanese have a great respect for them and, in old-fashioned inns, one often finds them hooded with fabric covers when not in use. He said: "Mirrors make a room uncozy." I am sure there is more to it than that although they love to be cozy. One must love coziness if one is to live so close together. But, as if in celebration of the thing they feared, they seemed to have made the entire city into a cold hall of mirrors which continually proliferated whole galleries of constantly changing appearances, all marvelous but none tangible. If they did not lock up the real looking-glasses, it would be hard to tell what was real and what was not. Even buildings one had taken for substantial had a trick of disappearing overnight. One morning, we woke to find the house next door reduced to nothing but a heap of sticks and a pile of newspapers neatly tied with string, left out for the garbage collector.

I would not say that he seemed to me to possess the same kind of insubstantiality although his departure usually seemed imminent, until I realized he was as erratic but as inevitable as the weather. If you plan to come and live in Japan, you must be sure you are stoical enough to endure the weather. No, it was not insubstantiality; it was a rhetoric valid only on its own terms. When I listened to his protestations, I was prepared to believe he believed in them, although I knew perfectly well they meant nothing. And that isn't fair. When he made them, he believed in them implicitly. Then, he was utterly consumed by conviction. But his dedication was primarily to the idea of himself in love. This idea seemed to him magnificent, even sublime. He was prepared to die for it, as one of Baudelaire's dandies might have been prepared to kill himself in order to preserve himself in the condition of a work of art, for he wanted to make this experience a masterpiece of experience which absolutely transcended the everyday. And this would annihilate the effects of the cruel drug, boredom, to which he was addicted although, perhaps, the element of boredom which is implicit in an affair so isolated from the real world was its principal appeal for him. But I had no means of knowing how far his conviction would take him. And I used to turn over in my mind from time to time the question: how far does a pretense of feeling, maintained with absolute conviction, become authentic?

This country has elevated hypocrisy to the level of the highest style. To look at a samurai, you would not know him for a murderer, or a geisha for a whore. The magnificence of such objects hardly pertains to the human. They live only in a world of icons and there they participate in rituals which transmute life itself to a series of grand gestures, as moving as they are absurd. It was as if they all thought, if we believe in something hard enough, it will come true and, lo and behold! they had and it did. Our street was in essence a slum but, in appearance, it was a little enclave of harmonious quiet and, *mirabile dictu,* it was the appearance which was the reality, because they all behaved so well, kept everything so clean and lived with such rigorous civility. What terrible discipline it takes to live harmoniously. They had crushed all their vigor in order to live harmoniously and now they had the wistful beauty of flowers pressed dry in an enormous book.

But repression does not necessarily give birth only to severe beauties. In its programmed interstices, monstrous passions bloom. They torture trees to make them look more like the formal notion of a tree. They paint amazing pictures on their skins with awl and gouge, sponging away the blood as they go; a tattooed man is a walking masterpiece of remembered pain. They boast the most passionate puppets in the world who mimic love suicides in a stylized fashion, for here there is no such comfortable formula as "happy ever after." And, when I remembered the finale of the puppet tragedies, how the wooden lovers cut their throats together, I felt the beginnings of unease, as if the hieratic imagery of the country might overwhelm me, for his boredom had reached such a degree that he was insulated against everything except the irritation of anguish. If he valued me as an object of passion, he had reduced the word to its root, which derives from the Latin, *patior*, I suffer. He valued me as an instrument which would cause him pain.

So we lived under a disoriented moon which was as angry a purple as if the sky had bruised its eye, and, if we made certain genuine intersections, these only took place in darkness. His contagious conviction that our love was unique and desperate infected me with an anxious sickness; soon we would learn to treat one another with the circumspect tenderness of comrades who are amputees, for we were surrounded by the most moving images of evanescence, fireworks, morning glories, the old, children. But the most moving of these images were the intangible reflections of ourselves we saw in one another's eyes, reflections of nothing but appearances, in a city dedicated to seeming, and, try as we might to possess the essence of each other's otherness, we would inevitably fail.

The Executioner's Beautiful Daughter

HERE, WE ARE HIGH in the uplands.

A baleful, almost-music, that of the tuneless cadences of an untutored orchestra repercussing in an ecstatic agony of echoes against the sounding boards of the mountains, lured us into the village square where we discover them twanging, plucking and abusing with horsehair bows a wide variety of crude, stringed instruments. Our feet crunch upon dryly whispering shifting sawdust freshly scattered over impacted surfaces of years of sawdusts clotted, here and there, with blood shed so long ago it has, with age, acquired the color and texture of rust . . . sad, ominous stains, a threat, a menace, memorials of pain.

There is no brightness in the air. Today the sun will not irradiate the heroes of the dark spectacle to which accident and disharmony combined to invite us. Here, where the air is choked all day with diffuse moisture tremulously, endlessly on the point of becoming rain, light falls as if filtered through muslin so at all hours a crepuscular gloaming prevails; the sky looks as though it is about to weep and so, gloomily illuminated through unshed tears, the *tableau vivant* before us is suffused with the sepia tints of an old photograph and nothing within it moves. The intent immobility of the spectators, wholly absorbed as they are in the performance of their hieratic ritual, is scarcely that of living things and this *tableau vivant* might be better termed a *nature morte* for the mirthless carnival is a celebration of a death. Their eyes, the whites of which are yellowish, are all fixed, as if attached by taut, invisible strings, upon a wooden block lacquered black with the spilt dews of a millennium of victims.

And now the rustic bandsmen suspend their unmelodious music. This death must be concluded in the most dramatic silence. The wild mountain-dwellers are gathered together to watch a public execution; that is the only entertainment the country offers.

Time, suspended like the rain, begins again in silence, slowly.

A heavy stillness ordering all his movements, the executioner himself adopts beside the block an offensively heroic pose, as if to do the thing with dignity were the only motive of the doing. He brings one booted foot to rest on the grim and sacrificial altar which is, to him, the canvas on which he exercises his art and proudly in his hand he bears his instrument, his axe.

The executioner stands more than six and a half feet high and he is broad to suit; the warped stumps of villagers gaze up at him with awe and fear. He is dressed always in mourning and always wears a curious mask. This mask is made of supple, close-fitting leather dyed an absolute black and it conceals his hair and the upper part of his face entirely except for two narrow slits through which issue the twin regards of eyes as inexpressive as though they were part of the mask. This mask reveals only his blunt-lipped, dark-red mouth and the grayish flesh which surrounds it. Laid out in such an unnerving fashion, these portions of his meat in no way fulfill the expectations we derive from our common knowledge of faces. They have a quality of obscene rawness as if, in some fashion, the lower face had been flayed. He, the butcher, might be displaying himself, as if he were his own meat.

Through the years, the close-fitting substance of the mask has become so entirely assimilated to the actual structure of his face that the face itself now seems to possess a parti-colored appearance, as if by nature dual; and this face no longer pertains to that which is human as if, when he first put on the mask, he blotted out his own, original face and so defaced himself forever. Because the hood of office renders the executioner an object. He has become an object who punishes. He is an object of fear. He is the image of retribution.

Nobody remembers why the mask was first devised nor who devised it. Perhaps some tender heart of antiquity adopted the concealing headgear in order to spare the one upon the block the sight of too human a face in the last moments of his agony; or else the origins of the article lie in a magical relation with the blackness of negation—

if, that is, negation is black in color. Yet the executioner dare not take off the mask in case, in a random looking-glass or, accidentally mirrored in a pool of standing water, he surprised his own authentic face. For then he would die of fright.

The victim kneels. He is thin, pale and graceful. He is twenty years old. The silent throng in the courtyard shudders in common anticipation; all their gnarled features twist in the same grin. No sound, almost no sound disturbs the moist air, only the ghost of a sound, a distant sobbing that might be the ululation of the wind amongst the scrubby pines. The victim kneels and lays his neck upon the block. Ponderously the executioner lifts his gleaming steel.

The axe falls. The flesh severs. The head rolls.

The cleft flesh spouts its fountains. The spectators shudder, groan and gasp. And now the string band starts to bow and saw again while a choir of stunted virgins, in the screeching wail that passes for singing in these regions, intones a barbaric requiem entitled: AWFUL WARNING OF THE SPECTACLE OF A DECAPITATION.

The executioner has beheaded his own son for committing the crime of incest upon the body of his sister, the executioner's beautiful daughter, on whose cheeks the only roses in these highlands grow.

Gretchen no longer sleeps soundly. After the day his decapitated head rolled in the bloody sawdust, her brother rode a bicycle interminably through her dreams even though the poor child crept out secretly, alone, to gather up the poignant, moist, bearded strawberry, his surviving relic, and take it home to bury beside her hen coop before the dogs ate it. But no matter how hard she scrubbed her little white apron against the scouring stones in the river, she could not wash away the stains that haunted the weft and warp of the fabric like pinkish phantoms of very precious fruit. Every morning, when she goes out to collect ripe eggs for her father's breakfast, she waters with felt but ineffectual tears the disturbed earth where her brother's brains lie rotting, while the indifferent hens peck and cluck about her feet.

This country is situated at such a high altitude water never boils, no matter how deceptively it foams within the pan, so their boiled eggs are always raw. The executioner insists his breakfast omelette be prepared only from those eggs precisely on the point of blossoming into chicks and, promptly at eight, consumes with relish a yellow, feathered omelette subtly spiked with claw. Gretchen, his tenderhearted daughter, often jumps and starts to hear the thwarted cluck from a still gelid, scarcely calcified beak about to be choked with sizzling butter, but her father, whose word is law because he never doffs his leather mask, will eat no egg that does not contain within it a nascent bird. That is his taste. In this country, only the executioner may indulge his perversities.

High among the mountains, how wet and cold it is! Chill winds blow soft drifts of rain across these almost perpendicular peaks; the wolf-haunted forests of fir and pine that cloak the lower slopes are groves fit only for the satanic cavortings of a universal Sabbath and a haunting mist pervades the bleak, meager villages rooted so far above quotidian skies a newcomer might not, at first, be able to breathe but only wheeze and choke in this thinnest of air. Newcomers, however, are less frequent apparitions than meteorites and thunderbolts; the villages breathe no welcome.

Even the walls of the rudely constructed houses exude suspicion. They are made from slabs of stone and do not have any windows to see out with. An inadequate orifice in the flat roof puffs out a few scant breaths of domestic smoke and penetration inside is effected only with the utmost difficulty through low, narrow doors, crevices in the granite, so each house presents to the eye as featureless a face as those of the Oriental demons whose anonymity was marred by no such commonplace a blemish as an eye, a nose or a mouth. Inside these ugly, unaccommodating hutches, man and domestic beast—goat, ox, pig, dog—stake equal squatting rights to the smoky and disordered hearths, although the dogs often grow rabid and rush frothing through the rutted streets like streams in spate.

The inhabitants are a thickset, sullen brood whose chronic malevolence stems from a variety of both environmental and constitutional causes. All share a general and unprepossessing cast of countenance. Their faces have the limp, flat, boneless aspect of the Eskimo and their eyes are opaque fissures since no eyelid hoods them, only the slack skin of the Mongolian fold. Their reptilian regards possess an intensity which is in no way intimate and their smiles are so peculiarly vicious it is all for the best they smile rarely. Their teeth rot young.

The men in particular are monstrously hirsute about both head and body. Their hair, a monotonous and uniform purplish black, grizzles, in age, to the tint of defunct ashes. Their womenfolk are built for durability rather than delight. Since all go always barefoot, the soles of their feet develop an intensifying consistency of horn from earliest childhood and the women, who perform all the tasks demanded by their primitive agriculture, sprout forearms the size and contour of vegetable marrows while their hands become pronouncedly scoop-shaped, until they resemble, in maturity, fat five-pronged forks.

All, without exception, are filthy and verminous. His shaggy head and rough garments are clogged with lice and quiver with fleas while his pubic areas throb and pulse with the blind convulsions of the crab. Impetigo, scabies and the itch are too prevalent among them to be remarked upon and their feet start early to decompose between the toes. They suffer from chronic afflictions of the anus due to their barbarous diet—thin porridge; sour beer; meat scarcely seared by the cool fires of the highlands; acidulated cheese of goat swallowed to the flatulent accompaniment of barley bread. Such comestibles cannot but contribute effectively to those disorders that have established the general air of malign unease which is their most immediately distinctive characteristic.

In this museum of diseases, the pastel beauty of Gretchen, the executioner's daughter, is all the more remarkable. Her flaxen plaits bob above her breasts as she goes to pluck, from their nests, the budding eggs.

Their days are shrouded troughs of glum manual toil and their nights wet, freezing, black, palpitating clefts gravid with the grossest cravings, nights dedicated solely to the imaginings of unspeakable desires tortuously conceived in mortified sensibilities habitually gnawed to suppuration by the black rats of superstition while the needle teeth of frost corrode their bodies.

They would, if they could, act out entire Wagnerian cycles of operatic evil and gleefully transform their villages into stages upon which the authentic monstrosities of Grand Guignol might be acted out in every unspeakable detail. No hideous parody of the delights of the flesh would be alien to them . . . *did they but know how such things were, in fact, performed.*

They have an inexhaustible capacity for sin but are inexorably balked by ignorance. They do not know what they desire. So their lusts exist in an undefined limbo, forever *in potentia.*

They yearn passionately after the most deplorable depravity but possess not the concrete notion of so much as a simple fetish, their tormented flesh betrayed eternally by the poverty of their imaginations and the limitations of their vocabulary, for how may one transmit such things in a language composed only of brute grunts and squawks representing, for example, the state of the family pig in labor? And, since their vices are, in the literal sense of the word, unspeakable, their secret, furious desires remain ultimately mysterious even to themselves and are contained only in the realm of pure sensation, or feeling undefined as thought or action and hence unrestrained by definition. So their desires are infinite, although, in real terms, except in the form of a prickle of perturbation, these desires could hardly be said to exist.

Their lives are dominated by a folklore as picturesque as it is murderous. Rigid, hereditary castes of wizards, warlocks, shamans and practitioners of the occult proliferate amongst these benighted mountain-dwellers and the apex of esoteric power lies, it would seem, in the person of the king himself. But this appearance is deceptive. This nominal ruler is in reality the poorest beggar in all his ragged kingdom. Heir of the barbarous, he is stripped of everything but the idea of an omnipotence which is sufficiently expressed by immobility.

All day long, ever since his accession, he depends by the right ankle from an iron ring set in the roof of a stone hut. A stout ribbon binds him to the ceiling and he is inadequately supported in a precarious but absolute position sanctioned by ritual and memory upon his left wrist, which is strapped in a similar fashion with ribbon to an iron ring cemented into the floor. He stays as still as if he had been dipped in a petrifying well and never speaks one single word because he has forgotten how.

They all believe implicitly they are damned. A folktale circulates among them, as follows: that the tribe was originally banished from a happier and more prosperous region to their present dreary habitation, a place fit only for continuous self-mortification, after they rendered themselves abhorrent to their former neighbors by the wholesale and enthusiastic practice of incest, son with father, father with daughter, etc.—every baroque variation possible upon the determinate quadrille of the nuclear family. In this country, incest is a capital crime; the punishment for incest is decapitation.

Daily their minds are terrified and enlightened by the continuous performances of apocalyptic dirges for fornicating siblings and only the executioner himself, because there is nobody to cut off his head, dare, in the immutable privacy of his leathern hood, upon his blood-bespattered block make love to his beautiful daughter.

Gretchen, the only flower of the mountains, tucks up her white apron and waltzing gingham skirts so they will not crease or soil but, even in the last extremity of the act, her father does not remove his mask for who would recognize him without it? The price he pays for his position is always to be locked in the solitary confinement of his power.

He perpetrates his inalienable right in the reeking courtyard upon the block where he struck off the head of his only son.

The Loves of Lady Purple

INSIDE THE PINK-STRIPED BOOTH of the Asiatic Professor only the marvelous existed and there was no such thing as daylight.

The puppet-master is always dusted with a little darkness. In direct relation to his skill, he propagates the most bewildering enigmas, for the more lifelike his marionettes, the more godlike his manipulations and the more radical the symbiosis between inarticulate doll and articulating fingers. The puppeteer speculates in a no-man's-limbo between the real and that which, although we know very well it is not, nevertheless seems to be real. He is the intermediary between us, his audience, the living, and they, the dolls, the undead, who cannot live at all and yet who mimic the living in every detail since, though they cannot speak or weep, still they project those signals of signification we instantly recognize as language.

The master of marionettes vitalizes inert stuff with the dynamics of his self. The sticks dance, make love, pretend to speak and, finally, personate death; yet, so many Lazaruses out of their graves they spring again in time for the next performance and no worms drip from their noses nor dust clogs their eyes. All complete, they once again offer their brief imitations of men and women with an exquisite precision which is all the more disturbing because we know it to be false; and so this art, if viewed theologically, may, perhaps, be subtly blasphemous.

Although he was only a poor traveling showman, the Asiatic Professor had become a consummate virtuoso of puppetry. He transported his collapsible theater, the cast of his single drama and a variety of properties in a horse-drawn cart and, after he played his play in many beautiful cities which no longer exist, such as Shanghai, Constantinople and St. Petersburg, he and his small entourage arrived at last in a country in Middle Europe where the mountains sprout jags as sharp and unnatural as those a child outlines with his crayon, a dark, superstitious Transylvania where they wreathed suicides with garlic, pierced them through the heart with stakes and buried them at crossroads while warlocks continually practiced rites of immemorial beastliness in the forests.

He had only the two assistants, a deaf boy in his teens, his nephew, to whom he taught his craft, and a foundling dumb girl no more than seven or eight they had picked up on their travels. When the Professor spoke, nobody could understand him for he knew only his native tongue, which was an incomprehensible rattle of staccato k's and t's, so he did not speak at all in the ordinary course of things and, if they had taken separate paths to silence, all, in the end, signed a perfect pact with it. But, when the Professor and his nephew sat in the sun outside their booth in the mornings before performances, they held interminable dialogues in sign language punctuated by soft, wordless grunts and whistles so that the choreographed quiet of their discourse was like the mating dance of tropic birds. And this means of communication, so delicately distanced from humanity, was peculiarly apt for the Professor, who had rather the air of a visitant from another world where the mode of being was conducted in nuances rather than affirmatives. This was due partly to his extreme age, for he was very old although he carried his years lightly even if, these days, in this climate, he always felt a little chilly and so wrapped himself always in a molting, woolen shawl; yet, more so, it was caused by his benign indifference to everything except the simulacra of the living he himself created.

Besides, however far the entourage traveled, not one of its members had ever comprehended to any degree the foreign. They were all natives of the fairground and, after all, all fairs are the same. Perhaps every single fair is no more than a dissociated fragment of one single, great, original fair which was inexplicably scattered long ago in a diaspora of the amazing. Whatever its location, a fair maintains its invariable, self-consistent atmosphere. Hieratic as knights in chess, the painted horses on the roundabouts describe perpetual circles as immutable as those of the planets and as immune to the drab world of here and now whose inmates come to gape at such extraordinariness, such freedom from actuality. The huckster's raucous invitations are made in a language beyond language, or, perhaps, in that ur-language of grunt and bark which lies behind all language. Everywhere, the same old women hawk glutinous candies which seem devised only to make flies drunk on sugar and, though the outward form of such excessive sweets may vary from place to place, their nature, never. A universal cast of two-headed dogs, dwarfs, alligator men, bearded ladies and giants in leopard-skin loincloths reveal their singularities in the sideshows and, wherever they come from, they share the sullen glamour of deformity, an internationality which acknowledges no geographic boundaries. Here, the grotesque is the order of the day.

The Asiatic Professor picked up the crumbs that fell from this heaping table yet never seemed in the least at home there for his affinities did not lie with its harsh sounds and primary coloring although it was the only home he knew. He had the wistful charm of a Japanese flower which only blossoms when dropped in water for he, too, revealed his passions through a medium other than himself and this was his didactic vedette, the puppet, Lady Purple.

She was the Queen of Night. There were glass rubies in her head for eyes and her ferocious teeth, carved out of mother-of-pearl, were always on show for she had a permanent smile. Her face was as white as chalk because it was covered with the skin of supplest white leather, which also clothed her torso, jointed limbs and complication of extremities. Her beautiful hands seemed more like weapons because her nails were so long, five inches of pointed tin enameled scarlet, and she wore a wig of black hair arranged in a chignon more heavily elaborate than any human neck could have endured. This monumental *cheve-*

lure was stuck through with many brilliant pins tipped with pieces of broken mirror so that, every time she moved, she cast a multitude of scintillating reflections which danced about the theater like mice of light. Her clothes were all of deep, dark, slumbrous colors—profound pinks, crimson and the vibrating purple with which she was synonymous, a purple the color of blood in a love suicide.

She must have been the masterpiece of a long-dead, anonymous artisan and yet she was nothing but a curious structure until the Professor touched her strings, for it was he who filled her with necromantic vigor. He transmitted to her an abundance of the life he himself seemed to possess so tenuously and, when she moved, she did not seem so much a cunningly simulated woman as a monstrous goddess, at once preposterous and magnificent, who transcended the notion she was dependent on his hands and appeared wholly real and yet entirely other. Her actions were not so much an imitation as a distillation and intensification of those of a born woman and so she could become the quintessence of eroticism, for no woman born would have dared to be so blatantly seductive.

The Professor allowed no one else to touch her. He himself looked after her costumes and jewelry. When the show was over, he placed his marionette in a specially constructed box and carried her back to the lodging house where he and his children shared a room, for she was too precious to be left in the flimsy theater and, besides, he could not sleep unless she lay beside him.

The catchpenny title of the vehicle for this remarkable actress was: *The Notorious Amours of Lady Purple, the Shameless Oriental Venus.* Everything in the play was entirely exotic. The incantatory ritual of the drama instantly annihilated the rational and imposed upon the audience a magic alternative in which nothing was in the least familiar. The series of tableaux which illustrated her story were in themselves so filled with meaning that when the Professor chanted her narrative in his impenetrable native tongue, the compulsive strangeness of the spectacle was enhanced rather than diminished. As he crouched above the stage directing his heroine's movements, he recited a verbal recitative in a voice which clanged, rasped and swooped up and down in a weird duet with the stringed instrument from which the dumb girl struck peculiar intervals. But it was impossible to mistake him when the Professor spoke in the character of Lady Purple herself for then his voice modulated to a thick, lascivious murmur like fur soaked in honey which sent unwilling shudders of pleasure down the spines of the watchers. In the iconography of the melodrama, Lady Purple stood for passion and all her movements were calculations in an angular geometry of sexuality.

The Professor somehow always contrived to have a few handbills printed off in the language of the country where they played. These always gave the title of his play and then they used to read as follows:

Come and see all that remains of Lady Purple, the famous prostitute and wonder of the East!

A unique sensation. See how the unappeasable appetites of Lady Purple turned her at last into the very puppet you see before you, pulled only by the strings of *lust*. Come and see the very doll, the only surviving relic of the shameless Oriental Venus herself.

The bewildering entertainment possessed almost a religious intensity for, since there can be no spontaneity in a puppet drama, it always tends towards the rapt intensity of ritual, and, at its conclusion, as the audience stumbled from the darkened booth, it had almost suspended disbelief and was more than half convinced, as the Professor assured them so eloquently, that the bizarre figure who had dominated the stage was indeed the petrification of a universal whore and had once been a woman in whom too much life had negated life itself, whose kisses had withered like acids and whose embrace blasted like lightning. But the Professor and his assistants immediately dismantled the scenery and put away the dolls, who were, after all, only mundane wood, and, next day, the play was played again.

This is the story of Lady Purple as performed by the Professor's puppets to the delirious *obbligato* of the dumb girl's samisen and the audible click of the limbs of the actors.

* * *

The Notorious Amours
of Lady Purple
the Shameless Oriental Venus

When she was only a few days old, her mother wrapped her in a tattered blanket and abandoned her on the doorstep of a prosperous merchant and his barren wife. These respectable *bourgeois* were to become the siren's first dupes. They lavished upon her all the attentions which love and money could devise and yet they reared a flower which, although perfumed, was carnivorous. At the age of twelve, she seduced her foster-father. Utterly besotted with her, he trusted to her the key of the safe where he kept all his money and she immediately robbed it of every farthing.

Packing his treasure in a laundry basket together with the clothes and jewelry he had already given her, she then stabbed her first lover and his wife, her foster mother, in their bellies with a knife used in the kitchen to slice fish. Then she set fire to their house to cover the traces of her guilt. She annihilated her own childhood in the blaze that destroyed her first home and, springing like a corrupt phoenix from the pyre of her crime, she rose again in the pleasure quarters, where she at once hired herself out to the madame of the most imposing brothel.

In the pleasure quarters, life passed entirely in artificial day for the bustling noon of those crowded alleys came at the time of drowsing midnight for those who lived outside that inverted, sinister, abominable world which functioned only to gratify the whims of the senses. Every rococo desire the mind of man might, in its perverse ingenuity, devise found ample gratification here, among the halls of mirrors, the flagellation parlors, the cabarets of nature-defying copulations and the ambiguous soirées held by men-women and female men. Flesh was the speciality of every house and it came piping hot, served up with all the garnishes imaginable. The Professor's puppets dryly and perfunctorily performed these tactical maneuvers like toy soldiers in a mock battle of carnality.

Along the streets, the women for sale, the mannequins of desire, were displayed in wicker cages so that potential customers could saunter past inspecting them at leisure. These exalted prostitutes sat motionless as idols. Upon their real features had been painted symbolic abstractions of the various aspects of allure and the fantastic elaboration of their dress hinted it covered a different kind of skin. The cork heels of their shoes were so high they could not walk but only totter and the sashes round their waists were of brocade so stiff the movements of the arms were cramped and scant so they presented attitudes of physical unease which, though powerfully moving, derived partly, at least, from the deaf assistant's lack of manual dexterity, for his apprenticeship had not as yet reached even the journeyman stage. Therefore the gestures of these hetaerae were as stylized as if they had been clockwork. Yet, however fortuitously, all worked out so well it seemed each one was as absolutely circumscribed as a figure in rhetoric, reduced by the rigorous discipline of her vocation to the nameless essence of the idea of woman, a metaphysical abstraction of the female which could, on payment of a specific fee, be instantly translated into an oblivion either sweet or terrible, depending on the nature of her talents.

Lady Purple's talents verged on the unspeakable. Booted, in leather, she became a mistress of the whip before her fifteenth birthday. Subsequently, she graduated into the mysteries of the torture chamber, where she thoroughly researched all manner of ingenious mechanical devices. She utilized a baroque apparatus of funnel, humiliation, syringe, thumbscrew, contempt and spiritual anguish; to her lovers, such severe usage was both bread and wine and a kiss from her cruel mouth was the sacrament of suffering.

Soon she became successful enough to be able to maintain her own establishment. When she was at the height of her fame, her slightest fancy might cost a young man his patrimony and, as soon as she squeezed him dry of fortune, hope and dreams, for she was quite remorseless, she abandoned him; or else she might, perhaps, lock him up in her closet and force him to watch her while she took for nothing to her usually incredibly expensive bed a beggar encountered by chance on the street. She was no malleable, since frigid, substance upon which desires might be executed; she was not a true prostitute for she was the object on which men prostituted themselves. She, the sole perpetrator of desire, proliferated malign fantasies all around her and used her lovers as the canvas on which she executed boudoir masterpieces of destruction. Skins melted in the electricity she generated.

Soon, either to be rid of them or, simply, for pleasure, she took to murdering her lovers. From the leg of a politician she poisoned she cut out the thighbone and took it to a craftsman who made it into a flute for her. She persuaded succeeding lovers to play tunes for her on this instrument and, with the supplest and most serpentine grace, she danced for them to its unearthly music. At this point, the dumb girl put down her samisen and took up a bamboo pipe from which issued weird cadences and, though it was by no means the climax of the play, this dance was the apex of the Professor's performance for the numinous pavane progressed like waves of darkness and, as she stamped, wheeled and turned to the sound of her malign chamber music, Lady Purple became entirely the image of irresistible evil.

She visited men like a plague, both bane and terrible enlightenment, and she was as contagious as the plague. The final condition of all her lovers was this: they went clothed in rags held together with the discharge of their sores, and their eyes held an awful vacancy, as if their minds had been blown out like candles. A parade of ghastly specters, they trundled across the stage, their passage implemented by medieval horrors for, here, an arm left its socket and whisked up out of sight into the flies and, there, a nose hung in the air after a gaunt shape that went tottering noseless forward.

So foreclosed Lady Purple's pyrotechnical career, which ended as if it had been indeed a firework display, in ashes, desolation and silence. She became more ghastly than those she had infected. Circe at last became a swine herself and, seared to the bone by her own flame, walked the pavements like a desiccated shadow. Disaster obliterated her. Cast out with stones and oaths by those who had once adulated her, she was reduced to scavenging on the seashore, where she plucked hair from the heads of the drowned to sell to wigmakers who catered to the needs of more fortunate since less diabolic courtesans.

Now her finery, her paste jewels and her enormous superimposition of black hair hung up in the green room and she wore a drab rag of coarse hemp for the final scene of her desperate decline, when, outrageous nymphomaniac, she practiced extraordinary necrophilies on the bloated corpses the sea tossed contemptuously at her feet for her dry rapacity had become entirely mechanical and still she repeated her former actions though she herself was utterly other. She abrogated her humanity. She became nothing but wood and hair. She became a marionette herself, herself her own replica, the dead yet moving image of the shameless Oriental Venus.

The Professor was at last beginning to feel the effect of age and travel. Sometimes he complained in noisy silence to his nephew of pains, aches, stiffening muscles, tautening sinews, and shortness of breath. He began to limp a little and left to the boy all the rough work of mantling and dismantling. Yet the balletic mime of Lady Purple grew all the more remarkable with the passage of the years as though his energy, channeled for so long into a single purpose, refined itself more and more in time and was finally reduced to a single, purified, concentrated essence which was transmitted entirely to the doll; and the Professor's mind attained a condition not unlike that of the swordsman trained in Zen, whose sword is his soul, so that neither sword nor swordsman has meaning without the presence of the other. Such swordsmen, armed, move towards their victims like automata, in a state of perfect emptiness, no longer aware of any distinction between self or weapon. Master and marionette had arrived at this condition.

Age could not touch Lady Purple for, since she had never aspired to mortality, she effortlessly transcended it and, though a man who was less aware of the expertise it needed to make her so much as raise her left hand might now and then, have grieved to see how she defied aging the Professor had no fancies of that kind. Her miraculous inhumanity rendered their friendship entirely free from the anthropomorphic, even on the night of the Feast of All Hallows when, the mountain-dwellers murmured, the dead held masked balls in the graveyards while the devil played the fiddle for them.

The rough audience received their copeck's worth of sensation and filed out into a fairground which still roared like a playful tiger with life. The foundling girl put away her samisen and swept out the booth while the nephew set the stage afresh for next day's matinee. Then the Professor noticed Lady Purple had ripped a seam in the drab shroud she wore in the final act. Chattering to himself with displeasure, he undressed her as she swung idly, this way and that way, from her anchored strings and then he sat down on a wooden property stool on the stage and plied his needle like a good housewife. The task was more difficult than it seemed at first for the fabric was also torn and required an embroidery of darning so he told his assistants to go home together to the lodging house and let him finish his task alone.

A small oil lamp hanging from a nail at the side of the stage cast an insufficient but tranquil light. The white puppet glimmered fitfully through the mists which crept into the theater from the night outside through all the chinks and gaps in the tarpaulin and now began to fold their chiffon drapes around her as if to decorously conceal her or else to render her more translucently enticing. The mist softened her painted smile a little and her head dangled to one side. In the last act, she wore a loose, black wig, the locks of which hung down as far as her softly upholstered flanks, and the ends of her hair flickered with her random movements, creating upon the white blackboard of her back one of those fluctuating optical effects which make us question the veracity of our vision. As he often did when he was alone with her, the Professor chatted to her in his native language, rattling away an intimacy of nothings, of the weather, of his rheumatism, of the unpalatability and expense of the region's coarse, black bread, while the small winds took her as their partner in a scarcely perceptible *valse triste* and the mist grew minute by minute thicker, more pallid and more viscous.

The old man finished his mending. He rose and, with a click or two of his old bones, he went to put the forlorn garment neatly on its green room hanger beside the glowing, winey purple gown splashed with rosy peonies, sashed with carmine, that she wore for her appalling dance. He was about to lay her, naked, in her coffin-shaped case and carry her back to their chilly bedroom when he paused. He was seized with the childish desire to see her again in all her finery once more that night. He took her dress off its hanger and carried it to where she drifted, at nobody's volition but that of the wind. As he put her clothes on her, he murmured to her as if she were a little girl for the vulnerable flaccidity of her arms and legs made a six-foot baby of her.

"There, there, my pretty; this arm here, that's right! Oops a daisy, easy does it . . ."

Then he tenderly took off her penitential wig and clucked his tongue to see how defenselessly bald she was beneath it. His arms cracked under the weight of her immense chignon and he had to stretch up on tiptoe to set it in place because, since she was as large as life, she was rather taller than he. But then the ritual of apparelling was over and she was complete again.

Now she was dressed and decorated, it seemed her dry wood had all at once put out an entire springtime of blossoms for the old man alone to enjoy. She could have acted as the model for the most beautiful of women, the image of that woman whom only memory and imagination can devise, for the lamplight fell too mildly to sustain her air of arrogance and so gently it made her long nails look as harmless as ten fallen petals. The Professor had a curious habit; he always used to kiss his doll good night.

A child kisses its toy before he pretends it sleeps although, even though he is only a child, he knows its eyes are not constructed to close so it will always be a sleeping beauty no kiss will waken. A man wistfully kisses the cheek of a grown daughter whose mind has not grown with her, even if he knows the touch of his lips is to her only that of some kind of fly which has briefly settled on her cheek. One in the grip of savage loneliness might kiss the face he sees before him in the mirror for want of any other face to kiss. All these are kisses of the same kind; they are the most poignant of caresses, for they are too humble and too despairing to wish or seek for any response.

Yet, in spite of the Professor's sad humility, his chapped and withered mouth opened on hot, wet, palpitating flesh.

The sleeping wood had wakened. Her pearl teeth crashed against his with the sound of cymbals and her warm, fragrant breath blew around him like an Italian gale. Across her suddenly moving face flashed a whole kaleidoscope of expression, as though she were running instantaneously through the entire repertory of human feeling, practicing, in an endless moment of time, all the scales of emotion as if they were music. Crushing vines, her arms curled about the Professor's delicate apparatus of bone and skin with the insistent pressure of an actuality by far more authentically living than that of his own, time-desiccated flesh. Her kiss emanated from the dark country where desire is objectified and lives. She gained entry into the world by a mysterious loophole in its metaphysics and, during her kiss, she sucked his breath from his lungs so that her own bosom heaved with it.

So, unaided, she began her next performance with an apparent improvisation which was, in reality, only a variation upon a theme. She sank her teeth into his throat and drained him. He did not have the time to make a sound. When he was empty, he slipped straight out of her embrace down to her feet with a dry rustle, as of a cast armful of dead leaves, and there he sprawled on the floorboards, as empty, useless and bereft of meaning as his own tumbled shawl.

She tugged impatiently at the strings which moored her and out they came in bunches from her head, her arms and her legs. She stripped them off her fingertips and stretched out her long, white hands, flexing and unflexing them again and again. For the first time for years, or, perhaps, forever, she closed her bloodstained teeth thankfully, for her cheeks still ached from the smile her maker had carved into the stuff of her former face. She stamped her elegant feet to make the new blood flow more freely there.

Unfurling and unraveling itself, her hair leapt out of its confinements of combs, cords and lacquer to root itself back into her scalp like cut grass bounding out of the stack and back again into the ground. First, she shivered with pleasure to feel the cold, for she realized she was experiencing a physical sensation; then either she remembered or else she believed she remembered that the sensation of cold was not a pleasurable one so she knelt and, drawing off the old man's shawl, wrapped it carefully about herself. Her every motion was instinct with a wonderful, reptilian liquidity. The mist outside now seemed to rush like a tide into the booth and broke against her in white breakers so that she looked like a baroque figurehead, lone survivor of a shipwreck, thrown up on a shore by the tide.

But whether she was renewed or newly born, returning to life or becoming alive, awakening from a dream or coalescing into the form of a fantasy generated in her wooden skull by the mere repetition so many times of the same invariable actions, the brain beneath the reviving hair contained only the scantiest notion of the possibilities now open to it. All that had seeped into the wood was the notion that she might perform the forms of life not so much by the skill of another as by her own desire that she did so, and she did not possess enough equipment to comprehend the complex circularity of the logic which inspired her for she had only been a marionette. But, even if she could not perceive it, she could not escape the tautological paradox in which she was trapped; had the marionette all the time parodied the living or was she, now living, to parody her own performance as a marionette? Although she was now manifestly a woman, young and extravagantly beautiful, the leprous whiteness of her face gave her the appearance of a corpse animated solely by demonic will.

Deliberately, she knocked the lamp down from its hook on the wall. A puddle of oil spread at once on the boards of the stage. A little flame leapt across the fuel and immediately began to eat the curtains. She went down the aisle between the benches to the little ticket booth. Already, the stage was an inferno and the corpse of the Professor tossed this way and that on an uneasy bed of fire. But she did not look behind her after she slipped out into the fairground although soon the theater was burning like a paper lantern ignited by its own candle.

Now it was so late that the sideshows, gingerbread stalls and liquor booths were locked and shuttered and only the moon, half obscured by drifting cloud, gave out a meager, dirty light, which sullied and deformed the flimsy pasteboard facades, so the place, deserted with curds of vomit, the refuse of revelry underfoot, looked utterly desolate.

She walked rapidly past the silent roundabouts, accompanied only by the fluctuating mists, towards the town, making her way like a homing pigeon, out of logical necessity, to the single brothel it contained.

The Smile of Winter

BECAUSE THERE ARE no seagulls here, the only sound is the resonance of the sea. This coastal region is quite flat, so that an excess of sky bears down with an intolerable weight, pressing the essence out of everything beneath it for it imposes such a burden on us that we have all been forced inward on ourselves in an introspective somberness intensified by the perpetual abrasive clamor of the sea. When the sun goes down, it is very cold and then I easily start crying because the winter moon pierces my heart. The winter moon is surrounded by an extraordinary darkness, the logical antithesis of the supernal clarity of the day; in this darkness, the dogs in every household howl together at the sight of a star, as if the stars were unnatural things. But, from morning until evening, a hallucinatory light floods the shore and a cool, glittering sun transfigures everything so brilliantly that the beach looks like a desert and the ocean like a mirage.

But the beach is never deserted. Far from it. At times, there is even a silent crowd of people—women who come in groups to turn the fish they have laid out to dry on bamboo racks; Sunday trippers; solitary anglers, even. Sometimes trucks drive up and down the beach to and fro from the next headland and after school is over children come to improvise games of baseball with sticks and a dead crab delivered to them by the tide. The children wear peaked, yellow caps; their heads are perfectly round. Their faces are perfectly bland, the color as well as the shape of brown eggs. They giggle when they see me because I am white and pink while they themselves are such a serviceable, unanimous beige. Besides all these visitors, the motorcyclists who come at night have left deep grooves behind them in the sand as if to say: "I have been here."

When the shadows of the evening lie so thickly on the beach it looks as though nobody has dusted it for years, the motorcyclists come out. That is their favorite time. They have marked out a course among the dunes with red wooden pegs and ride round it at amazing speeds. They come when they please. Sometimes they come in the early morning but, most often, by owl light. They announce their presence with a fanfare of opened throttles. They grow their hair long and it flies out behind them like black flags, for the Japanese are as beautiful as the outriders of death in the film *Orphée*. I wish they were not so beautiful; if they were not so beautiful and so inaccessible to me, then I should feel less lonely, although, after all, I came here in order to be lonely.

The beach is full of the garbage of the ocean. The waves leave torn, translucent furls of polythene wrapping too tough for even this sea's iron stomach; chipped jugs that once held rice wine; single seaboots freighted with sand; broken beer bottles and, once, a brown dog stiff and dead washed up as far as the pine trees which, subtly warped by the weather, squat on their hunkers at the end of my garden, where the dry soil transforms itself to sand.

Already the pines are budding this year's cones. Each blunt, shaggy bough is tipped with a small, lightly furred growth just like the prick of a little puppy while the dry, brown cones of last year still cling to the rough stems though now these are so insecure a touch will bring them bounding down. But, all in all, the pines have a certain intransigence. They dig their roots into dry soil full of seashells and strain backwards in the wind that blows directly from Alaska. They are absolutely exposed to the weather and yet as indifferent as the weather. The indifference of this Decembral littoral suits my forlorn mood for I am a sad woman by nature, no doubt about that; how unhappy I should be in a happy world! This country has the most rigorous romanticism in the world and they think a woman who lives by herself should accentuate her melancholy with surroundings of sentimental dilapidation. I have read about all the abandoned lovers in their old books eating their hearts out like Mariana in so many moated granges; their gardens are overgrown with goosegrass and mugwort, their mud walls are falling to pieces and their carp pools scaled over with water lily pads. Everything combines with the forlorn mood of the châtelaine to procure a moving image of poignant desolation. In this country you do not need to think, but only to look, and soon you think you understand everything.

The old houses in the village are each one dedicated to seclusion and court an individual sequestered sadness behind the weather-stained, unpainted wooden shutters they usually keep closed. It is a gloomy, aridly aesthetic architecture based on the principle of perpetual regression. The houses are heavily shingled and the roofs are the shapes and colors of waves frozen on a gray day. In the mornings, they dismantle the outer screens to let fresh air blow through and, as you walk past, you can see that all the inner walls are also sliding screens, though this time of stiff paper, and you can glimpse endlessly receding perspectives of interiors in brownish tones, as if everything had been heavily varnished some time ago; and, though these perspectives can be altered at will, the fresh rooms they make when they shift the screens about always look exactly the same as the old rooms. And all the matted interiors are the same, anyway.

Through the gaping palings of certain fences, I some-times see a garden so harmoniously in tune with the time of year it looks forsaken. But sometimes all these fragile habitations of unpainted wood; and the still-lifes, or *natures mortes,* of rusting water pumps and withered chrysanthe-mums in backyards; and the discarded fishing boats pulled up on the sand and left to rot away—sometimes the whole village looks forsaken. This is, after all, the season of aban-donment, of the suspension of vitality, a long cessation of vigor in which we must cultivate our stoicism. Everything has put on the desolate smile of winter. Outside my shabby front door, I have a canal, like Mariana in a moated grange; beyond the skulking pines at the back, there is only the ocean. The winter moon pierces my heart. I weep.

But when I went out on the beach this morning with the skin on my face starched with dried tears so I could feel my cheeks crackle in the wind, I found the sea had washed me up a nice present—two pieces of driftwood. One was a forked chunk like a pair of wooden trousers and the other was a larger, grayish, frayed root the shape of the paw of a ragged lion. I collect driftwood and set it up among the pine trees in picturesque attitudes on the edge of the beach and then I strike a picturesque attitude myself beside them as I watch the constantly agitated waves, for here we all strike picturesque attitudes and that is why we are so beautiful. Sometimes I imagine that one night the riders will stop at the end of my garden and I will hear the heels of their boots crunch on the friable carpet of last year's shed cones and then there will be a hesitant rattle of knuckles on the seaward-facing door and they will wait in ceremonious silence until I come, for their bodies are only images.

My pockets always contain a rasping sediment of sand because I always fill them with shells when I go onto the beach. The vast majority of these shells are round, sculptural forms the color of a brown egg, with warm, creamy insides. They have a classical simplicity. The scarcely perceptible indentations of their surfaces flow together to produce a texture as subtly matt as that of a petal which is as satisfying to touch as Japanese skin. But there are also pure white shells heavily ridged on the outside but within of a marmoreal smoothness and these come in hinged pairs.

There is still a third kind of shell, though I find these less often. They are curlicued, shaped like turbans and dappled with pink, of a substance so thin the ocean easily grinds away the outer husk to lay bare their spiralline cores. They are often decorated with baroque, infinitesimal swags of calcified parasites. They are the smallest of all the shells but by far the most intricate. When I picked up one of those shells, I found it contained the bright pink, dried, detached limb of a tiny sea creature like a dehydrated memory. Sometimes a litter of dropped fish lies among the shells. Each fish reflects the sky with the absolute purity of a Taoist mirror.

The fish have fallen off the racks on which they have been put out to dry. These bamboo racks spread with fish stand on trestles all along the beach as if a feast was laid for the entire prefecture but nobody had come to eat it. Close to the village, there are whole paddocks filled with bamboo racks. In one of these paddocks, a tethered goat crops grass. The fish are as shiny as fish of tin and the size of my little finger. Once dried, they are packed in plastic bags and sold to flavor soup.

The women lay them out. They come every day to turn them and, when the fish are ready, they pile up the racks and carry them to the packing sheds. There are great numbers of these raucously silent, and well-muscled, intimidating women.

The cruel wind burns port-wine whorls on their dour, inexpressive faces. All wear dark or drab-colored trousers pinched in at the ankle and either short rubber boots or split-toed socks on their feet. A layer of jacket sweaters and a loose, padded, cotton jacket gives them a squat, top-heavy look, as if they would not fall over, only rock malevolently to and fro if you pushed them. Over their jackets, they wear short, immaculate aprons trimmed with coarse lace and they tie white babushkas around their heads or sometimes wind a kind of wimple over the ears and round the throat. They are truculent and aggressive. They stare at me with open curiosity tinged with hostility. When they laugh, they display treasuries of gold teeth and their hands are as hard as those of eighteenth-century prizefighters, who also used to pickle their fists in brine. They make me feel that either I or they are deficient in femininity and I suppose it must be I since most of them hump about an organic lump of baby on their backs, inside their coats. It seems that only women people the village because most of the men are out on the sea. Early in the morning, I go out to watch the winking and blinking of the fishing boats on the water, which, just before dawn, has turned a deep violet.

The moist and misty mornings after a storm obscure the horizon for then the ocean has turned into the sky and the wind and waves have realigned the contours of the dunes. The wet sand is as dark and more yieldingly solid than fudge and walking across a panful is a promenade in the Kingdom of Sweets. The waves leave behind them glinting striations of salt and forcibly mold the foreshore into the curvilinear abstractions of cliffs, bays, inlets, curvilinear tumuli like the sculpture of Arp. But the storms themselves are a raucous music and turn my house into an Aeolian xylophone. All night long, the wind bangs and rattles away at every wooden surface; the house is a sounding box and even on the quietest nights the paper windows let through the wind that rattles softly in the pines.

Sometimes the lights of the midnight riders scrawl brilliant hieroglyphs across the panes, especially on moonless nights, when I am alone in a landscape of extraordinary darkness, and I am a little frightened when I see their headlamps and hear their rasping engines for then they seem the spawn of the negated light and to have driven straight out of the sea, which is just as mysterious as the night, even, and also its perfect image, for the sea is an inversion of the known and occupies half, or more, of the world, just as night does; while different peoples also live in the countries of the night.

They all wear leather jackets bristling with buckles, and high-heeled boots. They cannot buy such gaudy apparel in the village because the village shops only sell useful things such as paraffin, quilts and things to eat. And all the colors in the village are subfusc and equivocal, those of wood tinted bleakly by the weather and of lifeless wintry vegetation. When I sometimes see an orange tree hung with gold balls like a magic trick, it does nothing but stress by contrast the prevailing static sobriety of everything, which combines to smile in chorus the desolate smile of winter. On rainy nights when there is a winter moon bright enough to pierce the heart, I often wake to find my face still wet with tears so that I know I have been crying.

When the sun is low in the west, the beams become individually visible and fall with a peculiar, lateral intensity across the beach, flushing out long shadows from the grains of sand, and these beams seem to penetrate to the very hearts of the incoming waves which look, then, as if they were lit from within. Before they topple forward, they bulge outward in the swollen shapes and artfully flawed incandescence of Art Nouveau glass, as if the translucent bodies of the images they contain within them were trying to erupt, for the bodies of the creatures of the sea are images, I am convinced of that. At this time of day, the sea turns amazing colors—the brilliant, chemical green of the sea in nineteenth-century tinted postcards; or a blue far too cerulean for early evening; or sometimes it shines with such metallic brilliance I can hardly bear to look at it. Smiling my habitual winter smile, I stand at the end of my garden attended by a pack of green bears while I watch the constantly agitated white lace cuffs on the colorful sleeves of the Pacific.

Different peoples inhabit the countries of the ocean and some of their emanations undulate past me when I walk along the beach to the village on one of those rare, bleak, sullen days, spectral wraiths of sand blowing to various inscrutable meeting places on blind currents of the Alaskan wind. They twine around my ankles in serpentine caresses and they have eyes of sand but some of the other creatures have eyes of solid water and when the women move among trays of fish I think they, too, are sea creatures, spiny, ocean-bottom-growing flora, and if a tidal wave consumed the village—as it could do tomorrow, for there are no hills or seawalls to protect us—there, under the surface, life would go on just as before, the sea goat still nibbling, the shops still doing a roaring trade in octopus and pickled turnip greens, the women going about their silent business because everything is as silent as if it were under the water, anyway, and the very air is as heavy as water and warps the light so that one sees as if one's eyes were made of water.

Do not think I do not realize what I am doing. I am making a composition using the following elements: the winter beach; the winter moon; the ocean; the women; the pine trees; the riders; the driftwood; the shells; the shapes of darkness and the shapes of water; and the refuse. These are all inimical to my loneliness because of their indifference to it. Out of these pieces of inimical indifference, I intend to represent the desolate smile of winter which, as you must have gathered, is the smile I wear.

Penetrating to the Heart of the Forest

THE WHOLE REGION was like an abandoned flower bowl, filled to overflowing with green, living things; and, protected on all sides by the ferocious barricades of the mountains, those lovely reaches of forest lay so far inland the inhabitants believed the name, Ocean, that of a man in another country, and would have taken an oar, had they ever seen one, to be a winnowing fan. They built neither roads nor towns; in every respect like Candide, especially that of past ill-fortune, all they did now was to cultivate their gardens.

They were the descendants of slaves who, many years before, ran away from plantations in distant plains, in pain and hardship crossed the arid neck of the continent, and endured an infinity of desert and tundra, before they clambered the rugged foothills to scale at last the heights themselves and so arrive in a region that offered them in plentiful fulfillment all their dreams of a promised land. Now, the groves that skirted those forests of pine in the central valley formed for them all of the world they wished to know and nothing in their self-contained quietude concerned them but the satisfaction of simple pleasures. Not a single exploring spirit had ever been curious enough to search to its source the great river that watered their plots, or to penetrate to the heart of the forest itself. They had grown far too contented in their lost fastness to care for anything but the joys of idleness.

They had brought with them as a relic of their former life only the French their former owners had branded on their tongues, though certain residual, birdlike flutings of forgotten African dialects put unexpected cadences in their speech and, with the years, they had fashioned an arboreal argot of their own to which a French grammar would have proved a very fallible guide. And they had also packed up in their ragged bandanas a little, dark, voodoo folklore. But such bloodstained ghosts could not survive in sunshine and fresh air and emigrated from the villages in a body, to live only the ambiguous life of horned rumors in the woods, becoming at last no more than shapes with indefinable outlines who lurked, perhaps, in the green deeps, until, at last, one of the shadows modulated imperceptibly into the actual shape of a tree.

Almost as if to justify to themselves their lack of a desire to explore, they finally seeded by word of mouth a mythic and malign tree within the forest, a tree the image of the

Upas Tree of Java whose very shadow was murderous, a tree that exuded a virulent sweat of poison from its moist bark and whose fruits could have nourished with death an entire tribe. And the presence of this tree categorically forbade exploration—even though all knew, in their hearts, that such a tree did not exist. But, even so, they guessed it was safest to be a stay-at-home.

Since the woodlanders could not live without music, they made fiddles and guitars for themselves with great skill and ingenuity. They loved to eat well so they stirred themselves enough to plant vegetables, tend goats and chickens and blend these elements together in a rustic but voluptuous cuisine. They dried, candied and preserved in honey some of the wonderful fruits they grew and exchanged this produce with the occasional traveler who came over the single, hazardous mountain pass, carrying bales of cotton fabrics and bundles of ribbons. With these, the women made long skirts and blouses for themselves and trousers for their menfolk, so all were dressed in red and yellow flowered cloth, purple and green checkered cloth, or cloth striped like a rainbow, and they plaited themselves hats from straw. They needed nothing more than a few flowers before they felt their graceful toilets were complete and a profusion of flowers grew all around them, so many flowers that the straw-thatched villages looked like inhabited gardens, for the soil was of amazing richness and the flora proliferated in such luxuriance that when Dubois, the botanist, came over the pass on his donkey, he looked down on that paradisial landscape and exclaimed: "Dear God! It is as if Adam had opened Eden to the public!"

Dubois was seeking a destination whose whereabouts he did not know, though he was quite sure it existed. He had visited most of the out-of-the-way parts of the world to peer through the thick lenses of his round spectacles at every kind of plant. He gave his name to an orchid in Dahomey, to a lily in Indochina and to a dark-eyed Portuguese girl in a Brazilian town of such awesome respectability that even its taxis wore antimacassars. But, because he loved the frail wife whose grave eyes already warned him she would live briefly, he rooted there, a plant himself in alien soil, and, out of gratitude, she gave him two children at one birth before she died.

He found his only consolation in a return to the flowering wilderness he had deserted for her sake. He was approaching middle age, a rawboned, bespectacled man who habitually stooped out of a bashful awareness of his immense height, hirsute and gentle as a herbivorous lion. The vicissitudes of a life in which his reticence had cheated him of the fruits of his scholarship, together with the forlorn conclusion of his marriage, had left him with a yearning for solitude and a desire to rear his children in a place where ambition, self-seeking and guile were strangers, so that they would grow up with the strength and innocence of young trees.

But such a place was hard to find.

His wanderings took him to regions ever more remote from civilization but he was never seized with a conviction of homecoming until that morning, as the sun irradiated the mists and his donkey picked its way down a rough path so overgrown with dew-drenched grass and mosses it had become no more than the subtlest intimation of a direction.

It took him circuitously down to a village sunk in a thicket of honeysuckle that filled with languorous sweetness the rarefied air of the uplands. On the dawning light hung, trembling, the notes of a pastoral aubade somebody was picking out on a guitar. As Dubois passed the house, a plump, dark-skinned woman with a crimson handkerchief round her head threw open a pair of shutters and leaned out to pick a spray of morning glory. As she tucked it behind her ear, she saw the stranger and smiled like another sunrise, greeting him with a few melodious phrases of his native language she had somehow mixed with burned cream and sunshine. She offered him a little breakfast which she was certain he must need since he had traveled so far and, while she spoke, the yellow-painted door burst open and a chattering tide of children swept out to surround the donkey, turning up to Dubois faces like sunflowers.

Six weeks after his arrival among the Creoles, Dubois left again for the house of his parents-in-law. There, he packed his library, notebooks and records of researches; his most precious collections of specimens and his equipment; as much clothing as he felt would last him the rest of his life and a crate containing objects of sentimental value. This case and his children were the only concessions he made to the past. And, once he had installed all those things safely in a wooden farmhouse the villagers had interrupted their inactivity long enough to make ready for him, he closed the doors of his heart to everything but the margins of the forest, which were to him a remarkable book it would take all the years that remained to him to learn to read.

The birds and beasts showed no fear of him. Painted magpies perched reflectively on his shoulders as he pored over the drawings he made among the trees, while fox cubs rolled in play around his feet and even learned to nose in his capacious pockets for cookies. As his children grew older, he seemed to them more an emanation of their surroundings than an actual father, and from him they unknowingly imbibed a certain radiant inhumanity which sprang from a benign indifference towards by far the greater part of mankind—towards all those who were not beautiful, gentle and, by nature, kind.

"Here, we have all become *homo silvester,* men of the woods," he would say. "And that is by far superior to the precocious and destructive species, *homo sapiens*—knowing man. Knowing man, indeed; what more than nature does man need to know?"

Careless brown children were their playfellows and their toys were birds, butterflies and flowers. Their father spared them enough of his time to teach them to read, to write and to draw. Then he gave them the run of his library and left them alone, to grow as they pleased. So they thrived on a diet of simple food, warm weather, perpetual holidays and haphazard learning. They were fearless since there was nothing to be afraid of and they always spoke the truth because there was no need to lie. No hand or voice was ever raised in anger against them and so they did not know what anger was; when they came across the word in books, they thought it must mean the mild fretfulness they felt when it rained two days together, which did not happen often. They quite forgot the dull town where they had been born. The green world took them for its own and they were fitting children of their foster-mother, for they were strong, lithe and supple, browned by the sun to the very color of the villagers whose liquid patois they spoke. They resembled one another so closely each could have used the other as a mirror and almost seemed to be different aspects of the same person for all their gestures, turns of phrase and manners of speech were exactly similar. Had they known how, they would have been proud, because their intimacy was so perfect it could have bred that sense of loneliness which is the source of pride and, as they read more and more of their father's books, their companionship deepened since they had nobody but one another with whom to discuss the discoveries they made in common. From morning to evening, they were never apart, and at night they slept together in a plain, narrow bed on a floor of beaten earth while the window held the friendly nightlight of a soft, southern moon above them in a narrow frame. But often they slept under the moon itself, for they came and went as they pleased and spent most of their time out of doors, exploring the forests until they had gone further and seen more than ever their father had.

At last, these explorations took them into the untrodden, virginal reaches of the deep interior. Here, they walked hand in hand beneath the vaulted architraves of pines in a hushed interior like that of a sentient cathedral. The topmost branches twined so thickly that only a subdued viridian dazzle of light could filter through and the children felt against their ears a palpable fur of intense silence. Those who felt less kinship with the place might have been uneasy, as if abandoned among serene, voiceless, giant forms that cared nothing for man. But, if the children sometimes lost their way, they never lost themselves for they took the sun by day and the stars by the otherwise trackless night for their compass and could discern clues in the labyrinth that those who trusted the forest less would not have recognized, for they knew the forest too well to know of any harm it might do them.

Long ago, in their room at home, they began work on a map of the forest. This was by no means the map an authentic cartographer would have made. They marked hills with webs or feathers of the birds they found there, clearings with an integument of pressed flowers and especially magnificent trees with delicate, brightly colored drawings on whose water-color boughs they stuck garlands of real leaves so that the map became a tapestry made out of the substance of the forest itself. At first, in the center of the map, they put their own thatched cottage and Madeline drew in the garden the shaggy figure of their father, whose leonine mane was as white, now, as the puffball of a dandelion, bending with a green watering can over his pots of plants, tranquil, beloved and oblivious. But as they grew older, they grew discontented with their work for they found out their home did not lie at the heart of the forest but only somewhere in its green suburbs. They were seized with the desire to pierce more and yet more deeply into the unfrequented places and now their expeditions lasted for a week or longer. Though he was always glad to see them return, their father had often forgotten they had been away. At last, nothing but the discovery of the central node of the unvisited valley, the navel of the forest, would satisfy them. It grew to be almost an obsession with them. They spoke of the adventure only to one another and did not share it with the other companions who, as they grew older, grew less and less necessary to their absolute intimacy, since, lately, for reasons beyond their comprehension, this intimacy had been subtly invaded by tensions which exacerbated their nerves yet exerted on them both an intoxicating glamour.

Besides, when they spoke of the heart of the forest to their other friends, a veil of darkness came over the woodlanders' eyes and, half-laughing, half-whispering, they would hint at the wicked tree that grew there as though, even if they did not believe in it, it was a metaphor for something unfamiliar they preferred to ignore, as one might say: "Let sleeping dogs lie. Aren't we happy as we are?" When they saw this laughing apathy, this incuriosity blended with a tinge of fear, Emile and Madeline could not help but feel a faint contempt, for their world, though beautiful, seemed to them, in a sense, incomplete—as though it lacked the knowledge of some mystery they might find, might they not? in the forest, on their own.

In their father's books they found references to the Antiar or Antshar of the Indomalay archipelago, the Antiaris Toxicaria whose milky juice contains a most potent poison, like the quintessence of belladonna. But their reason told them that not even the most intrepid migratory bird could have brought the sticky seeds on its feet to cast them down here in these landlocked valleys far from Java. They did not believe the wicked tree could exist in this hemisphere; and yet they were curious. But they were not afraid.

One August morning, when both were thirteen years old, they put bread and cheese in their knapsacks and started out on a journey so early the homesteads were sleeping and even the morning glories were still in bud. The settlements were just as their father had seen them first, prelapsarian villages where any Fall was inconceivable; his children, bred in those quiet places, saw them with eyes pure of nostalgia for lost innocence and thought of them only with that faint, warm claustrophobia which the word "home" signifies. At noon, they ate lunch with a family whose cottage lay at the edges of the uninhabited places and when they bade their hosts good-bye, they knew, with a certain anticipatory relish, they would not see anyone else but one another for a long time.

At first, they followed the wide river which led them directly into the ramparts of the great pines and, though days and nights soon merged together in a sonorous quiet where trees grew so close together that birds had no room to sing or fly, they kept a careful tally of the passing time for they knew that, five days away from home, along the leisurely course of the water, the pines thinned out.

The bramble-covered river banks, studded, at this season, with flat, pink discs of blossom, grew so narrow that the water tumbled fast enough to ring out various carillons while gray squirrels swung from branch to low branch of trees which, released from the strait confines of the forest, now grew in shapes of a feminine slightness and grace. Rabbits twitched moist, velvet noses and laid their ears along their backs but did not run away when they saw the barefoot children go by and Emile pointed out to Madeline how a wise toad, squatting meditatively among the kingcups, must have a jewel in his head because bright beams darted out through his eyes, as though a cold fire burned inside his head. They had read of this phenomenon in old books but never seen it before.

They had never seen anything in this place before. It was so beautiful they were a little awestruck.

Then Madeline stretched out her hand to pick a water lily unbudding on the surface of the river but she jumped back with a cry and gazed down at her finger with a mixture of pain, affront and astonishment. Her bright blood dripped down onto the grass.

"Emile!" she said. "It bit me!"

They had never encountered the slightest hostility in the forest before. Their eyes met in wonder and surmise while the birds chanted recitatives to the accompaniment of the river.

"This is a strange place," said Emile hesitantly. "Perhaps we should not pick any flowers in this part of the forest. Perhaps we have found some kind of carnivorous water lily."

He washed the tiny wound, bound it with his handkerchief and kissed her cheek, to comfort her, but she would not be comforted and irritably flung a pebble in the direction of the flower. When the pebble struck the lily, it unfurled its closed circle of petals with an audible snap and, bewildered, they glimpsed inside them a set of white, perfect fangs. Then the waxen petals closed swiftly over the teeth again, concealing them entirely, and the water lily again looked perfectly white and innocent.

"See! It *is* a carnivorous water lily!" said Emile. "Father *will* be excited when we tell him."

But Madeline, her eyes still fixed on the predator as if it fascinated her, slowly shook her head. She had grown very grave.

"No," she said. "We must not talk of the things we find in the heart of the forest. They are all secrets. If they were not secrets, we would have heard of them before."

Her words fell with a strange weight, as heavy as her own gravity, as if she might have received some mysterious communication from the perfidious mouth that wounded her. At once, listening to her, Emile thought of the legendary tree; and then he realized that, for the first time in his life, he did not understand her, for, of course, they had heard of the tree.

Looking at her in a new puzzlement, he sensed the ultimate difference of a femininity he had never before known any need or desire to acknowledge and this difference might give her the key to some order of knowledge to which he might not yet aspire, himself, for all at once she seemed far older than he. She raised her eyes and fixed on him a long, solemn regard which chained him in a conspiracy of secrecy, so that, henceforth, they would share only with one another the treacherous marvels round them. At last, he nodded.

"Very well, then," he said. "We won't tell father."

Though they knew he never listened when they spoke to him, never before had they consciously concealed anything from him.

Night was approaching. They walked a little further, until they found pillows of moss laid ready for their heads beneath the branches of a flowering hawthorn tree. They drank clear water, ate the last of the food they had brought with them and then slept in one another's arms as if they were the perfect children of the place, although they slept less peacefully than usual for both were visited by unaccustomed nightmares of knives and snakes and suppurating roses. But though each stirred and murmured, the dreams were so strangely inconsequential, nothing but fleeting sequences of detached, malign images, that the children forgot them as they slept and woke only with an irritable residue of nightmare, the dregs of unremembered dreaming, knowing only they had slept badly.

In the morning, they stripped and bathed in the river. Emile saw that time was subtly altering the contours of both their bodies and he found he could no longer ignore his sister's nakedness, as he had done since babyhood, while, from the way she suddenly averted her own eyes after, in her usual playful fashion, she splashed him with water, she, too, experienced the same extraordinary confusion. So they fell silent and hastily dressed themselves. And yet the confusion was pleasurable and made their blood sting. He examined her finger and found the marks of the lily's teeth were gone; the wound had healed over completely. Yet he still shuddered with an unfamiliar thrill of dread when he remembered the fanged flower.

"We have no food left," he said. "We should turn back at noon."

"Oh, no!" said Madeline with a mysterious purposefulness that might have been rooted, had he known it, only in a newborn wish to make him do as she wanted, against his own wishes. "No! I'm sure we shall find something to eat. After all, this is the season for wild strawberries."

He, too, knew the lore of the forest. At no time of the year could they not find food—berries, roots, salads, mushrooms, and so on. So he saw she knew he had only used a pale excuse to cover his increasing agitation at finding himself alone with her so far from home. And now he had used up his excuse, there was nothing for it but to go on. She walked with a certain irresolute triumph, as though she were aware she had won an initial victory which, though insignificant in itself, might herald more major battles in the future, although they did not even know the formula for a quarrel, yet.

And already this new awareness of one another's shapes

and outlines had made them less twinned, less indistinguishable from one another. So they fell once more to their erudite botanizing, in order to pretend that all was as it had always been, before the forest showed its teeth; and now the meandering path of the river led them into such magical places that they found more than enough to talk about for, by the time the shadows vanished at noon, they had come into a landscape that seemed to have undergone an alchemical change, a vegetable transmutation, for it contained nothing that was not marvelous.

Ferns uncurled as they watched, revealing fronded fringes containing innumerable, tiny, shining eyes glittering like brilliants where the ranks of seeds should have been. A vine was covered with slumbrous, purple flowers that, as they passed, sang out in a rich contralto with all the voluptuous wildness of flamenco—and then fell silent. There were trees that bore, instead of foliage, brown, speckled plumage of birds. And when they had grown very hungry, they found a better food than even Madeline had guessed they might, for they came to a clump of low trees with trunks scaled like trout, growing at the water's edge. These trees put out shell-shaped fruit and, when they broke these open and ate them, they tasted oysters. After they consumed their fishy luncheon, they walked on a little and discovered a tree knobbed with white, red-tipped whorls that looked so much like breasts they put their mouths to the nipples and sucked a sweet, refreshing milk.

"See?" said Madeline, and this time her triumph was unconcealed. "I told you we should find something to nourish us!"

When the shadows of the evening fell like a thick dust of powdered gold on the enchanted forest and they were beginning to feel weary, they came to a small valley which contained a pool that seemed to have no outlet or inlet and so must be fed by an invisible spring. The valley was filled with the most delightful, citronesque fragrance as sharply refreshing as a celestial eau-de-cologne and they saw the source of the perfume at once.

"Well!" exclaimed Emile. "This certainly isn't the fabled Upas Tree! It must be some kind of incense tree, such as the incense trees of Upper India where, after all, one finds a similar climate, or so I've read."

The tree was a little larger than a common apple tree but far more graceful in shape. The springing boughs hung out a festival of brilliant streamers, long, aromatic sprays of green, starlike flowers tipped with the red anthers of the stamens, cascading over clusters of leaves so deep a green and of such a glossy texture the dusk turned them to discs of black glass, those that the sunset did not turn to fire. These leaves hid secret bunches of fruit, mysterious spheres of visible gold streaked with green, as if all the unripe suns in the world were sleeping on the tree until a multiple, universal dawning should wake them all in splendor. As they stood hand in hand, gazing at the beautiful tree, a small wind parted the leaves so they would see the fruit more clearly and, in the rind, set squarely in the middle of each faintly flushed cheek, was a curious formation—a round set of serrated indentations exactly resembling the marks of a bite made by the teeth of a hungry man. As if the sight stimulated her own appetite, Madeline laughed and said: "Goodness, Emile, the forest has even given us dessert!"

She sprang towards the exquisite, odoriferous tree which, at that moment, suffused in a failing yet hallucinatory light the tone and intensity of liquefied amber, seemed to her brother a perfect equivalent of his sister's amazing beauty, a beauty he had never seen before that filled him, now, with ecstasy. The dark pool reflected her darkly, like an antique mirror. She raised her hand to part the leaves in search of a ripe fruit but the greenish skin seemed to warm and glow under her fingers so the first one she touched came as easily off the stem as if it had been brought to perfection by her touch. It seemed to be some kind of apple or pear. It was so juicy the juice ran down her chin and she extended a long, crimson, newly sensual tongue to lick her lips, laughing.

"It tastes so good!" she said. "Here! Eat!"

She came back to him, splashing through the margins of the pool, holding the fruit out towards him on her palm. She was like a beautiful statue which has just come to life. Her enormous eyes were lit like nocturnal flowers that had been waiting only for this special night to open and, in their vertiginous depths, reveal to her brother in inexpressible entirety the hitherto unguessed at, unknowable, inexpressible vistas of love.

He took the apple; ate; and, after that, they kissed.

Flesh and the Mirror

It was midnight—I chose my times and set my scenes with the precision of the born artiste. Hadn't I gone eight thousand miles to find a climate with enough anguish and hysteria in it to satisfy me? I had arrived back in Yokohama that evening from a visit to England and nobody met me, although I expected him. So I took the train to Tokyo, half an hour's journey. First, I was angry; but the poignancy of my own situation overcame me and then I was sad. To return to the one you love and find him absent! My heart used to jump like Pavlov's dogs at the prospect of such a treat; I positively salivated at the suggestion of un- pleasure, I was sure that *that* was real life. I'm told I always look lonely when I'm alone; that is because, when I was an intolerable adolescent, I learned to sit with my coat collar turned up in a lonely way, so that people would talk to me. And I can't drop the habit even now, though, now, it's only a habit and, I realize, a predatory habit.

It was midnight and I was crying bitterly as I walked under the artificial cherry blossom with which they decorate the lamp standards from April to September. They do that so the pleasure quarters will have the look of a continuous carnival, no matter what ripples of agitation disturb the never-ceasing, endlessly circulating, quiet, gentle, melancholy crowds who throng the wet web of alleys under a false ceiling of umbrellas. All looked as desolate as Mardi Gras. I was searching among a multitude of unknown faces for the face of the one I loved while the warm, thick, heavy rain of summer greased the dark surfaces of the streets until, after a while, they began to gleam like sleek fur of seals just risen from the bottom of the sea.

The crowds lapped round me like waves full of eyes until I felt that I was walking through an ocean whose speechless and gesticulating inhabitants, like those with whom medieval philosophers peopled the countries of the deep, were methodical inversions or mirror images of the dwellers on dry land. And I moved through these expressionist perspectives in my black dress as though I was the creator of all and of myself, too, in a black dress, in love, crying, walking through the city in the third person singular, my own heroine, as though the world stretched out from my eye like spokes from a sensitized hub that galvanized all to life when I looked at it.

I think I know, now, what I was trying to do. I was trying to subdue the city by turning it into a projection of my own growing pains. What solipsistic arrogance! The city, the largest city in the world, the city designed to suit not one of my European expectations, this city presents the foreigner with a mode of life that seems to him to have the enigmatic transparency, the indecipherable clarity, of dream. And it is a dream he could, himself, never have dreamed. The stranger, the foreigner, thinks he is in control; but he has been precipitated into somebody else's dream.

You never know what will happen in Tokyo. Anything can happen.

I had been attracted to the city first because I suspected it contained enormous histrionic resources. I was always rummaging in the dressing-up box of the heart for suitable appearances to adopt in the city. That was the way I maintained my defenses for, at that time, I always used to suffer a great deal if I let myself get too close to reality since the definitive world of the everyday with its hard edges and harsh light did not have enough resonance to echo the demands I made upon experience. It was as if I never experienced experience *as* experience. Living never lived up to the expectations I had of it—the Bovary syndrome. I was always imagining other things that could have been happening, instead, and so I always felt cheated, always dissatisfied.

Always dissatisfied, even if, like a perfect heroine, I wandered, weeping, on a forlorn quest for a lost lover through the aromatic labyrinth of alleys. And wasn't I in Asia? Asia! But, even though I lived there, it always seemed far away from me. It was as if there were glass between me and the world. But I could see myself perfectly well on the other side of the glass. There I was, walking up and down, eating meals, having conversations, in love, indifferent, and so on. But all the time I was pulling the strings of my own puppet; it was this puppet who was moving about on the other side of the glass. And I eyed the most marvelous adventures with the bored eye of the agent with the cigar watching another audition. I tapped out the ash and asked of events: "What else can you do?"

So I attempted to rebuild the city according to the blueprint in my imagination as a backdrop to the plays in my puppet theater, but it sternly refused to be so rebuilt; I was only imagining it had been so rebuilt. On the night I came back to it, however hard I looked for the one I loved, she could not find him anywhere and the city delivered her into the hands of a perfect stranger who fell into step beside her and asked why she was crying. She went with him to an unambiguous hotel with a mirror on the ceiling and lascivious black lace draped round a palpably illicit bed. His eyes were shaped like sequins. All night long, a thin, pale, sickle moon with a single star pendant at its nether tip floated upon the rain that pitter-pattered against the windows and there was a clockwork whirring of cicadas. From time to time, the windbell dangling from the eaves let out an exquisitely mournful tinkle.

None of the lyrical eroticism of this sweet, sad, moon night of summer rain had been within my expectations; I had half expected he would strangle me. My sensibility wilted under the burden of response. My sensibility foundered under the assault on my senses.

My imagination had been preempted.

The room was a box of oiled paper full of the echoes of the rain. After the light was out, as we lay together, I could still see the single shape of our embrace in the mirror above me, a marvelously unexpected conjunction cast at random by the enigmatic kaleidoscope of the city. Our pelts were stippled with the fretted shadows of the lace curtains as if our skins were a mysterious uniform provided by the management in order to render all those who made love in that hotel anonymous. The mirror annihilated time, place and person; at the consecration of this house, the mirror had been dedicated to the reflection of chance embraces. Therefore it treated flesh in an exemplary fashion, with charity and indifference.

The mirror distilled the essence of all the encounters of strangers whose perceptions of one another existed only in the medium of the chance embrace, the accidental. During the durationless time we spent making love, we were not ourselves, whoever that might have been, but in some sense the ghosts of ourselves. But the selves we were not, the selves of our own habitual perceptions of ourselves, had a far more insubstantial substance than the reflections we were. The magic mirror presented me with a hitherto unconsidered notion of myself as I. Without any intention of mine, I had been defined by the action reflected in the mirror. I beset me. I was the subject of the sentence written on the mirror. I was not watching it. There was nothing whatsoever beyond the surface of the glass. Nothing kept me from the fact, the act; I had been precipitated into knowledge of the real conditions of living.

Mirrors are ambiguous things. The bureaucracy of the mirror issues me with a passport to the world; it shows me my appearance. But what use is a passport to an armchair traveler? Women and mirrors are in complicity with one another to evade the action I/she performs that she/I cannot watch, the action with which I break out of the mirror, with which I assume my appearance. But *this* mirror refused to conspire with me; it was like the first mirror

I'd ever seen. It reflected the embrace beneath it without the least guile. All it showed was inevitable. But I myself could never have dreamed it.

I saw the flesh and the mirror but I could not come to terms with the sight. My immediate response to it was to feel I'd acted out of character. The fancy-dress disguise I'd put on to suit the city had betrayed me to a room and a bed and a modification of myself that had no business at all in my life, not in the life I had watched myself performing.

Therefore I evaded the mirror. I scrambled out of its arms and sat on the edge of the bed and lit a fresh cigarette from the butt of the old one. The rain beat down. My demonstration of perturbation was perfect in every detail, just like the movies. I applauded it. I was gratified the mirror had not seduced me into behaving in a way I would have felt inappropriate—that is, shrugging and sleeping, as though my infidelity was not of the least importance. I now shook with the disturbing presentiment that he with his sequin eyes who'd been kind to me was an ironic substitute for the other one, the one I loved, as if the arbitrary carnival of the streets had gratuitously offered me this young man to find out if I *could* act out of character and then projected our intersection upon the mirror, as an objective lesson in the nature of things.

Therefore I dressed rapidly and ran away as soon as it was light outside, that mysterious, colorless light of dawn when the hooded crows flap out of the temple groves to perch on the telegraph poles, cawing a baleful dawn chorus to the echoing boulevards empty, now, of all the pleasure-seekers. The rain had stopped. It was an overcast morning so hot that I broke out into a sweat at the slightest movement. The bewildering electrographics of the city at night were all switched off. All the perspectives were pale, gritty gray, the air was full of dust. I never knew such a banal morning.

The morning before the night before, the morning before this oppressive morning, I woke up in the cabin of a boat. All the previous day, as we rounded the coast in bright weather, I dreamed of the reunion before me, a lovers' meeting refreshed by the three months I'd been gone, returning home due to a death in the family. I will come back as soon as I can—I'll write. Will you meet me at the pier? Of course, of course he will. But he was not at the pier; where was he?

So I went at once to the city and began my desolate tour of the pleasure quarters, looking for him in all the bars he used. He was nowhere to be found. I did not know his address, of course; he moved from rented room to rented room with the agility of the feckless and we had corresponded through accommodation addresses, coffee shops, poste restante, etc. Besides, there had been a displacement of mail reminiscent of the excesses of the nineteenth-century novel, such as it is difficult to believe and could only have been caused by a desperate emotional necessity to cause as much confusion as possible. Both of us prided ourselves on our passionate sensibilities, of course. That was *one* thing we had in common! So, although I thought I was the most romantic spectacle imaginable as I wandered weeping down the alleys, I was in reality at risk—I had fallen through one of the holes life leaves in it; these peculiar holes are the entrances to the counters at which you pay the price of the way you live.

Random chance operates in relation to these existential

lacunae; one tumbles down them when, for the time being, due to hunger, despair, sleeplessness, hallucination or those accidental-on-purpose misreadings of train timetables and airline schedules that produce margins of empty time, one is lost. One is at the mercy of events. That is why I like to be a foreigner; I only travel for the insecurity. But I did not know that, then.

I found my self-imposed fate, my beloved, quite early that morning but we quarreled immediately. We quarreled the day away assiduously and, when I tried to pull the strings of my self and so take control of the situation, I was astonished to find the situation I wanted was disaster, shipwreck. I saw his face as though it were in ruins, although it was the sight in the world I knew best and, the first time I saw it, had not seemed to me a face I did not know. It had seemed, in some way, to correspond to my idea of my own face. It had seemed a face long known and well remembered, a face that had always been imminent in my consciousness as an idea that now found its first visual expression.

So I suppose I do not know how he really looked and, in fact, I suppose I shall never know, now, for he was plainly an object created in the mode of fantasy. His image was already present somewhere in my head and I was seeking to discover it in actuality, looking at every face I met in case it was the right face—that is, the face which corresponded to my notion of the unseen face of the one I should love, a face created parthenogenetically by the rage to love which consumed me. So his self, and, by his self, I mean the thing he was to himself, was quite unknown to me. I created him solely in relation to myself, like a work of romantic art, an object corresponding to the ghost inside me. When I'd first loved him, I wanted to take him apart, as a child dismembers a clockwork toy, to comprehend the inscrutable mechanics of its interior. I wanted to see him far more naked than he was with his clothes off. It was easy enough to strip him bare and then I picked up my scalpel and set to work. But, since I was so absolutely in charge of the dissection, I only discovered what I was able to recognize already, from past experience, inside him. If ever I found anything new to me, I steadfastly ignored it. I was so absorbed in this work it never occurred to me to wonder if it hurt him.

In order to create the loved object in this way and to issue it with its certificate of authentication, as beloved, I had also to labor at the idea of myself in love. I watched myself closely for all the signs and, precisely upon cue, here they were! Longing, desire, self-abnegation, etc. I was racked by all the symptoms. Even so, in spite of this fugue of feeling, I had felt nothing but pleasure when the young man who picked me up inserted his sex inside me in the blue-movie bedroom. I only grew guilty later, when I realized I had not felt in the least guilty at the time. And was I in character when I felt guilty or in character when I did not? I was perplexed. I no longer understood the logic of my own performance. My script had been scrambled behind my back. The cameraman was drunk. The director had a *crise de nerfs* and been taken away to a sanatorium. And my co-star had picked himself up off the operating table and painfully cobbled himself together again according to his own design! All this had taken place while I was looking at the mirror.

Imagine my affront.

We quarreled until night fell and, still quarreling, found

our way to another hotel but this hotel, and this night, was in every respect a parody of the previous night. (That's more like it! Squalor and humiliation! Ah!) Here, there were no lace drapes nor windbells nor moonlight nor any moist whisper of lugubriously seductive rain; this place was bleak, mean and cheerless and the sheets on the mattress they threw down on the floor for us were blotched with dirt although, at first, we did not notice that because it was necessary to pretend the urgent passion we always used to feel in one another's presence even if we felt it no longer, as if to act out the feeling with sufficient intensity would re-create it by sleight of hand, although our skins (which knew us better than we knew ourselves) told us the period of reciprocation was over. It was a mean room and the windows overlooked a parking lot with a freeway beyond it, so that the paper walls shuddered with the reverberations of the infernal clamor of the traffic. There was a sluggish electric fan with dead flies caught in the spokes and a single strip of neon overhead lit us and everything up with a scarcely tolerable, quite remorseless light. A slatternly woman in a filthy apron brought us glasses of thin, cold, brown tea made from barley and then she shut the door on us. I would not let him kiss me between the thighs because I was afraid he would taste the traces of last night's adventure, a little touch of paranoia in *that* delusion.

I don't know how much guilt had to do with the choice of this décor. But I felt it was perfectly appropriate.

The air was thicker than tea that's stewed on the hob all day and cockroaches were running over the ceiling, I remember. I cried all the first part of the night, I cried until I was exhausted but he turned on his side and slept—

he saw through that ruse, though I did not since I did not know that I was lying. But I could not sleep because of the rattling of the walls and the noise of traffic. We had turned off the glaring lamp; when I saw a shaft of light fall across his face, I thought: "Surely it's too early for the dawn." But it was another person silently sliding open the unlocked door; in this disreputable hotel, anything can happen. I screamed and the intruder vanished. Wakened by a scream, my lover thought I'd gone mad and instantly trapped me in a stranglehold, in case I murdered him.

We were both old enough to have known better, too.

When I turned on the lamp to see what time it was, I noticed, to my surprise, that his features were blurring, like the underwriting on a palimpsest. It wasn't long before we parted. Only a few days. You can't keep *that* pace up for long.

Then the city vanished; it ceased, almost immediately, to be a magic and appalling place. I woke up one morning and found it had become home. Though I still turn up my coat collar in a lonely way and am always looking at myself in mirrors, they're only habits and give no clue at all to my character, whatever that is.

The most difficult performance in the world is acting naturally, isn't it? Everything else is artful.

Master

AFTER HE DISCOVERED that his vocation was to kill animals, the pursuit of it took him far away from temperate weather until, in time, the insatiable suns of Africa eroded the pupils of his eyes, bleached his hair and tanned his skin until he no longer looked the thing he had been but its systematic negative; he became the white hunter, victim of an exile which is the imitation of death, a willed bereavement. He would emit a ravished gasp when he saw the final spasm of his prey. He did not kill for money but for love.

He had first exercised a propensity for savagery in the acrid lavatories of a minor English public school where he used to press the heads of the new boys into the ceramic bowl and then pull the flush upon them to drown their gurgling protests. After puberty, he turned his indefinable but exacerbated rage upon the pale, flinching bodies of young women whose flesh he lacerated with teeth, fingernails and sometimes his leather belt in the beds of cheap hotels near London's great rail termini (King's Cross, Victoria, Euston . . .). But these pastel-colored excesses, all the cool, rainy country of his birth could offer him, never satisfied him; his ferocity would attain the coloring of the fauves only when he took it to the torrid zones and there refined it until it could be distinguished from that of the beasts he slaughtered only by the element of self-consciousness it retained, for, if little of him now pertained to the human, the eyes of his self still watched him so that he was able to applaud his own depredations.

Although he decimated herds of giraffe and gazelle as they grazed in the savannahs until they learned to snuff their annihilation upon the wind as he approached, and dispatched heraldically plated hippopotami as they lolled up to their armpits in ooze, his rifle's particular argument lay with the silken indifference of the great cats, and, finally, he developed a speciality in the extermination of the printed beasts, leopards and lynxes, who carry ideograms of death in the clotted language pressed in brown ink upon their pelts by the fingertips of mute gods who do not acknowledge any divinity in humanity.

When he had sufficiently ravaged the cats of Africa, a country older by far than we are, yet to whose innocence he had always felt superior, he decided to explore the nether regions of the New World, intending to kill the painted beast, the jaguar, and so arrived in the middle of a metaphor for desolation, the place where time runs back on itself, the moist, abandoned cleft of the world whose fructifying river is herself a savage woman, the Amazon. A green, irrevocable silence closed upon him in that serene kingdom of giant vegetables. Dismayed, he clung to the bottle as if it were a teat.

He traveled by jeep through an invariable terrain of architectonic vegetation where no wind lifted the fronds of palms as ponderous as if they had been sculpted out of viridian gravity at the beginning of time and then abandoned, whose trunks were so heavy they did not seem to rise into the air but, instead, drew the oppressive sky down upon the forest like a coverlid of burnished metal. These tree trunks bore an outcrop of plants, orchids, poisonous, iridescent blossoms and creepers the thickness of an arm with flowering mouths that stuck out viscous tongues to trap the flies that nourished them. Bright birds of unknown shapes infrequently darted past him and sometimes monkeys, chattering like the third form, leaped from branch to branch that did not move beneath them. But no motion nor sound did more than ripple the surface of the profound, inhuman introspection of the place so that, here, to kill became the only means that remained to him to confirm he himself was still alive, for he was not prone to introspection and had never found any consolation in nature. Slaughter was his only proclivity and his unique skill.

He came upon the Indians who lived among the lugubrious trees. They represented such a diversity of ethnic types they were like a living museum of man organized on a principle of regression for, the further inland he went, the more primitive they became, as if to demonstrate that evolution could be inverted. Some of the brown men had no other habitation than the sky and, like the flowers, ate insects; they would paint their bodies with the juice of leaves and berries and ornament their heads with diadems of feathers or the claws of eagles. Placid and decorative, the men and women would come softly twittering around his jeep, a mild curiosity illuminating the inward-turning, amber suns of their eyes, and he did not recognize that they were men although they distilled demented alcohol in stills of their own devising and he drank it, in order to people the inside of his head with familiar frenzy among so much that was strange.

His half-breed guide would often take one of the brown girls who guilelessly offered him her bare, pointed breasts and her veiled, limpid smile and, then and there, infect her with the clap to which he was a chronic martyr in the bushes at the rim of the clearing. Afterwards, licking his chops with remembered appetite, he would say to the hunter: Brown meat, brown meat. In drunkenness one night, troubled by the prickings of a carnality that often visited him at the end of his day's work, the hunter bartered, for the spare tire of his jeep, a pubescent girl as virgin as the forest that had borne her.

She wore a vestigial slip of red cotton twisted between her thighs and her long, sinuous back was upholstered in cut velvet, for it was whorled and ridged with the tribal markings incised on her when her menses began—raised designs like the contour map of an unknown place. The women of her tribe dipped their hairs in liquid mud and then wound their locks into long curls around sticks and let them dry in the sun until each one possessed a chevelure of rigid ringlets the consistency of baked, unglazed pottery, so she looked as if her head was surrounded by one of those spiked haloes allotted to famous sinners in Sunday-school picture books. Her eyes held the gentleness and the despair of those about to be dispossessed; she had the immovable smile of a cat, which is forced by physiology to smile whether it wants to or not.

The beliefs of her tribe had taught her to regard herself as a sentient abstraction, an intermediary between the ghosts and the fauna, so she looked at her purchaser's fever-shaking, skeletal person with scarcely curiosity, for he was to her no more yet no less surprising than any other gaunt manifestation of the forest. If she did not perceive him as a man, either, that was because her cosmogony admitted no essential difference between herself and the beasts and the spirits, it was so sophisticated. Her tribe never killed; they only ate roots. He taught her to eat the meat he roasted over his campfire and, at first, she did not like it much but dutifully consumed it as though he were ordering her to partake of a sacrament for, when she saw how casually he killed the jaguar, she soon realized he was death itself. Then she began to look at him with wonder for she recognized immediately how death had glorified itself to become the principle of his life. But when he looked at her, he saw only a piece of curious flesh he had not paid much for.

He thrust his virility into her surprise and, once her wound had healed, used her to share his sleeping bag and carry his pelts. He told her her name would be Friday, which was the day he bought her; he taught her to say "master" and then let her know that was to be his name. Her eyelids fluttered for, though she could move her lips and tongue and so reproduce the sounds he made, she did not understand them. And, daily, he slaughtered the jaguar. He sent away the guide for, now he had bought the girl, he did not need him; so the ambiguous lovers went on together, while the girl's father made sandals from the rubber tire to shoe his family's feet and they walked a little way into the twentieth century in them, but not far.

Among her tribe circulated the following picturesque folktale. The jaguar invited the anteater to a juggling contest in which they would use their eyes to play with, so they drew their eyes out of the sockets. When they had finished, the anteater threw his eyes up into the air and back they fell—plop! in place in his head; but when the jaguar imitated him, his eyes caught in the topmost branches of a tree and he could not reach them. So he became blind. Then the anteater asked the macaw to make new eyes out of water for the jaguar and, with these eyes, the jaguar found that it could see in the dark. So all turned out well for the jaguar; and she, too, the girl who did not know her own name, could see in the dark. As they moved always more deeply into the forest, away from the little settlements, nightly he extorted his pleasure from her flesh and she would gaze over her shoulder at shapes of phantoms in the thickly susurrating undergrowth, phantoms—it seemed to her—of beasts he had slaughtered that day, for she had been born into the clan of the jaguar and, when his leather belt cut her shoulder, the magic water of which her eyes were made would piteously leak.

He could not reconcile himself to the rain forest, which oppressed and devastated him. He began to shake with malaria. He killed continually, stripped the pelts and left the corpses behind him for the vultures and the flies.

Then they came to a place where there were no more roads.

His heart leaped with ecstatic fear and longing when

he saw how nothing but beasts inhabited the interior. He wanted to destroy them all, so that he would feel less lonely, and, in order to penetrate this absence with his annihilating presence, he left the jeep behind at a forgotten township where a green track ended and an ancient whiskey priest sat all day in the ruins of a forsaken church brewing firewater from wild bananas and keening the stations of the cross. Master loaded his brown mistress with his guns and the sleeping bag and the gourds filled with liquid fever. They left a wake of corpses behind them for the plants and the vultures to eat.

At night, after she lit the fire, he would first abuse her with the butt of his rifle about the shoulders and, after that, with his sex; then drink from a gourd and sleep. When she had wiped the tears from her face with the back of her hand, she was herself again, and, after they had been together a few weeks, she seized the opportunity of solitude to examine his guns, the instruments of his passion, and, perhaps, learn a little of Master's magic.

She squinted her eye to peer down the long barrel; she caressed the metal trigger, and, pointing the barrel carefully away from her as she had seen Master do, she softly squeezed it in imitation of his gestures to see if she, too, could provoke the same shattering exhalation. But, to her disappointment, she provoked nothing. She clicked her tongue against her teeth in irritation. Exploring further, however, she discovered the secret of the safety catch.

Ghosts came out of the jungle and sat at her feet, cocking their heads on one side to watch her. She greeted them with a friendly wave of her hand. The fire began to fail but she could see clearly through the sights of the rifle since her eyes were made of water and, raising it to her shoulder as she had seen Master do, she took aim at the disc of moon stuck to the sky beyond the ceiling of boughs above her, for she wanted to shoot the moon down since it was a bird in her scheme of things and, since he had taught her to eat meat, now she thought she must be death's apprentice.

He woke from sleep in a paroxysm of fear and saw her, dimly illuminated by the dying fire, naked but for the rag that covered her sex, with the rifle in her hand; it seemed to him her clay-covered head was about to turn into a nest of birds of prey. She laughed delightedly at the corpse of the sleeping bird her bullet had knocked down from the tree and the moonlight glimmered on her curiously pointed teeth. She believed the bird she shot down had been the moon and now, in the night sky, she saw only the ghost of the moon. Though they were lost, hopelessly lost, in the trackless forest, she knew quite well where she was; she was always at home in the ghost town.

Next day, he oversaw the beginnings of her career as a markswoman and watched her tumble down from the boughs of the forest representatives of all the furred and feathered beings it contained. She always gave the same delighted laugh to see them fall for she had never thought it would be so easy to populate her fireside with fresh ghosts. But she could not bring herself to kill the jaguar, since the jaguar was the emblem of her clan; with forceful gestures of her head and hands, she refused. But, after she learned to shoot, soon she became a better hunter than he although there was no method to her killing and they went banging away together indiscriminately through the dim, green undergrowth.

The descent of the banana spirit in the gourd marked

the passage of time and they left a gross trail of carnage behind them. The spectacle of her massacres moved him and he mounted her in a frenzy, forcing apart her genital lips so roughly the crimson skin on the inside bruised and festered while the bites on her throat and shoulders oozed diseased pearls of pus that brought the blowflies buzzing about her in a cloud. Her screams were a universal language; even the monkeys understood she suffered when Master took his pleasure, yet he did not. As she grew more like him, so she began to resent him.

While he slept, she flexed her fingers in the darkness that concealed nothing from her and, without surprise, she discovered her fingernails were growing long, curved, hard and sharp. Now she could tear his back when he inflicted himself upon her and leave red runnels in his skin; yelping with delight, he only used her the more severely and, twisting her head with its pottery appendages this way and that in pained perplexity, she gouged the empty air with her claws.

They came to a spring of water and she plunged into it in order to wash herself but she sprang out again immediately because the touch of water aroused such an unpleasant sensation on her pelt. When she impatiently tossed her head to shake away the waterdrops, her clay ringlets melted altogether and trickled down her shoulders. She could no longer tolerate cooked meat but must tear it raw between her fingers off the bone before Master saw. She could no longer twist her scarlet tongue around the two syllables of his name, "mas-tuh"; when she tried to speak, only a diffuse and rumbling purr shivered the muscles of her throat and she dug neat holes in the earth to bury her excrement, she had become so fastidious since she grew whiskers.

Madness and fever consumed him. When he killed the jaguar, he abandoned them in the forest with the stippled pelts still on them. To possess the clawed she was in itself a kind of slaughter, and, tracking behind her, his eyes dazed with strangeness and liquor, he would watch the way the intermittent dentellation of the sun through the leaves mottled the ridged tribal markings down her back until they seemed the demarcations of blotched areas of pigmentation subtly mimicking the beasts who mimicked the patterns of the sun through the leaves and, if she had not walked upright on two legs, he would have shot her. As it was, he thrust her down into the undergrowth, among the orchids, and drove his other weapon into her soft, moist hole while he tore her throat with his teeth and she wept, until, one day, she found she was not able to cry any more.

The day the liquor ended, he was alone with fever. He reeled, screaming and shaking, in the clearing where she had abandoned his sleeping bag; she crouched among the lianas and crooned in a voice like soft thunder. Though it was daylight, the ghosts of innumerable jaguar crowded round to see what she would do. Their invisible nostrils twitched with the prescience of blood. The shoulder to which she raised the rifle now had the texture of plush.

His prey had shot the hunter, but now she could no longer hold the gun. Her brown and amber dappled sides rippled like water as she trotted across the clearing to worry the clothing of the corpse with her teeth. But soon she grew bored and bounded away.

Then only the flies crawling on his body were alive and he was far from home.

Reflections

I WAS WALKING in a wood one late spring day of skimming cloud and shower-tarnished sunshine, the sky a lucid if intermittent blue—cool, bright, tremulous weather. A coloratura blackbird perched on a bough curded with greenish mayblossom let fall a flawed chain of audible pearl; I was alone in the spring-enchanted wood. I slashed the taller grasses with my stick and now and then surprised some woodland creature, rat or rabbit, that fled away from me through long grass where little daisies and spindly branches of buttercups were secreted among gleaming stems still moist at the roots from last night's rain that had washed and refreshed the entire wood, had dowered it the poignant transparency, the unique, inconsolable quality of rainy countries, as if all was glimpsed through tears.

The crisp air was perfumed with wet grass and fresh earth. The year was swinging on the numinous hinges of the solstice but I was ingenuous and sensed no imminence in the magic silence of the rustling wood.

Then I heard a young girl singing. Her voice performed a trajectory of sound far more ornate than that of the blackbird, who ceased at once to sing when he heard it for he could not compete with the richly crimson sinuosity of a voice that pierced the senses of the listener like an arrow in a dream. She sang; and her words thrilled through me, for they seemed filled with a meaning that had no relation to meaning as I understood it.

"Under the leaves," she sang, "and the leaves of life—" Then, in mid-flight, the song ceased and left me dazzled. My attention abstracted from my surroundings, all at once my foot turned on an object hidden in the grass and I tumbled to the ground. Though I fell on the soft, wet grass, I was shaken and winded. I forgot that luring music. Cursing my obstacle, I searched among the pale, earth-stained rootlets to find it and my fingers closed on, of all things, a shell. A shell so far from the sea! When I tried to grasp it in order to pick it up and examine it the better, I found the act unexpectedly difficult and my determination to lift it quickened although, at the same time, I felt a shiver of fear for it was so very, very heavy and its contours so chill that a shock like cold electricity darted up my arm from the shell, into my heart. I was seized with the most intense disquiet; I was mystified by the shell.

I thought it must be a shell from a tropic ocean, since it was far larger and more elaborately whorled than the shells I'd found on the shores of the Atlantic. There was some indefinable strangeness in its shape I could not immediately define. It glimmered through the grass like a cone of trapped moonlight although it was so very cold and so heavy it seemed to me it might contain all the distilled heaviness of gravity itself within it. I grew very much afraid of the shell; I think I sobbed. Yet I was so determined to wrench it from the ground that I clenched my muscles and gritted my teeth and tugged and heaved. Up it came, at last, and I rolled over backwards when it freed itself. But now I held the prize in my hands, and I was, for the moment, satisfied.

When I looked at the shell more closely, I saw the nature of the teasing difference that had struck me when I first set eyes on it. The whorls of the shell went the wrong way. The spirals were reversed. It looked like the mirror image of a shell, and so it should not have been able to exist outside a mirror; in this world, it could not exist outside a mirror. But, all the same, I held it.

The shell was the size of my cupped hands and cold and heavy as death.

In spite of its fabulous weight, I decided to carry it through the wood for I thought I would take it to the little museum in the nearby town where they would inspect it and test it and tell me what it might be and how it could have arrived where I found it. But as I staggered along with it in my arms, it exerted such a pull downwards on me that, several times, I nearly fell to my knees, as if the shell were determined to drag me, not down to the earth but into the earth itself. And then, to complete my confusion, I heard that witching voice again.

"Under the leaves—"

But, this time, when a gasp stopped the song, the voice changed at once to the imperative.

"Sick 'im!" she urged. "Sick 'im!"

Before I had a chance to do more than glance in the direction of the voice, a bullet whirred over my head and buried itself in the trunk of an elm tree, releasing from their nests in the upward branches a whirring hurricane of crows. An enormous black dog bounded towards me from the undergrowth so suddenly I saw no more than his yawning scarlet maw and lolling tongue before I went down on my face beneath him. The fright nearly bereft me of my senses. The dog slavered wetly over me and, the next thing I knew, a hand seized my shoulder and roughly turned me over.

She had called the dog away and now it sat on its haunches, panting, watching me with a quick, red eye. It was black as coal, some kind of lurcher, with balls the size of grapefruit. Both the dog and the girl glanced at me without charity. She wore blue jeans and boots, a wide, vindictively buckled leather belt and a green sweater. Her tangled brown hair hung about her shoulders in a calculated disorder that was not wild. Her dark eyebrows were perfectly straight and gave her stern face a gravity as awful as that of the shell I held in my hand. Her blue eyes, the kind the Irish say have been put in with a sooty finger, held no comfort nor concern for me for they were the eyes that justice would have if she were not blind. She carried a sporting rifle slung across her shoulder and I knew at once this rifle had fired the shot. She might have been the gamekeeper's daughter but, no, she was too proud; she was a savage and severe wood-ranger.

Why I do not know, but every impulse told me to conceal my shell and I hugged it close to me, as if my life depended on keeping it, although it was so heavy and began to throb with a wild palpitation so that it seemed the shell had disordered my own heart, or else had become my own disordered heart. But my brusque captress poked at my hands with the barrel of her rifle so roughly my bruised fingers let the shell fall. She bent forward so that her necromantic hair brushed my face and picked up the shell with amazing ease.

She examined it for a moment and then, without a word or sign to me, tossed it to her lurcher, who seized it in his mouth ready to carry it for her. The dog began to wag his tail. The rhythmic swishing of his tail upon the grass was now the only sound in the clearing. Even the trees had ceased to murmur, as though a holy terror hushed them.

She gestured me to my feet and, when I was upright, she thrust the mouth of the gun in the small of my back and marched me through the wood at gunpoint, striding along behind me while the dog padded beside her with the shell in his mouth. All this took place in unadulterated silence, but for the raucous panting of the dog. The cabbage white butterflies flickered upon the still air as if nothing whatsoever were out of the ordinary, while delicious-looking apricot and violet colored clouds continued to chase one another across the sun according to the indifferent logic of the upper heavens, for the clouds were moved by a fierce wind that blew so high above the wood everything around me was as tranquil as water trapped in a lock, and mocked the inward perturbation that shook me.

Soon we reached an overgrown path that took us to a gate set in a garden wall where there was an old-fashioned bellpull and, dangling above it, a bell stained with moss and rust. The girl with the rifle rang this bell before she opened the gate as if to warn whoever was at home that visitors were arriving. The gate led into a graceful and dilapidated walled garden full of the herbaceous splendors of early summer, hollyhocks, wallflowers, roses. There was a mossed sundial and a little stone statue of a nude youth stretching his arms up out of a cuirass of ivy. But, though the bees hummed among the flower-bells, the grass was as long as it had been in the wood and just as full of buttercups and daisies. Dandelions expired in airy seed-heads in the flower beds; ragged robin and ground elder conspired to oust the perennials from the borders and a bright sadness of neglect touched everything as though with dust, just as it did the ancient brick house, almost covered with creepers, that slept within the garden, an ancient, tumbledown place with a look of oracular blindness in windows that were stopped up with vines and flowers. The roof was lichened quite over, so that it seemed upholstered in sleek, green fur. Yet there was no peace in the disheveled loveliness of the place; the very plants that grew there seemed tensed in a curious expectancy, as though the garden were a waiting-room. There was a short, crumbling flight of steps that led to a weathered front door, ajar like the door of a witch's house.

Before the door, I involuntarily halted; a dreadful vertigo seized me, as if I stood on the edge of an abyss. My heart had been thumping far too hard and far too fast since I had picked up the shell and now it seemed about to burst from too much strain. Faintness and terror of death swept over me; but the girl prodded me cruelly in the buttocks with her rifle so I was forcibly marched into a country-house hall with dark stained floorboards, a Persian carpet and a Jacobean oak chest with an antique bowl on it, all complete yet all as if untouched for years, for decades. A maze of dust danced in the beam of sunshine that disturbed the choked indoor air when we broke into it. Every corner was softened by cobwebs while the industrious spiders had wound filaments of geometric lace this way and that between the crumbling furniture. A sweet, rank smell of damp and decay filled the house; it was cold inside, and dark. The door swung to behind us but did not close and we went up a staircase of worm-eaten oak, I first, she after and then the dog, whose claws clattered on the bare wood.

At first I thought the spiders had cast their nets on both sides of the stair but then I saw the workmanship that wound down the inner side of the staircase was not that of the spiders for, though it was the same color, this web had a determinate pattern that resembled nothing so much as openwork knitting, the kind of featherlike, floating stuff from which they make courtesans' bedjackets. This knitting was part of an interminable muffler that, as I watched it, crept, with vegetable slowness, little by little downstairs towards the hall. Yard upon yard of the muffler was coiled up in airy folds on the landing and there I could hear the clack, clack, clack of a pair of knitting needles ticking away monotonously near at hand. The muffler came out of a door that, like the front door, stood a little open; it edged through the gap like a tenuous serpent.

My captress motioned me aside with the muzzle of her rifle and knocked firmly on the door.

Inside the room, someone coughed dryly, then invited us: "Come in."

It was a soft, rustling, unemphatic, almost uninflected, faded, faintly perfumed voice, like very old lace handkerchiefs put away long ago in a drawer with potpourri and forgotten.

My captress thrust me though the door before her; when I was close to her, my nostrils quivered at the vicious odor of her skin. It was a large room, part drawing-room, part bedroom, for the being who lived in it was crippled. She, he, it—whoever, whatever my host or hostess may have been—lay in an old-fashioned wicker bathchair beside a cracked marble fireplace bossed with swags and cupids. Her white hands finished in fingers so indecently long, so white and so translucent they raised lewd thoughts of candles and feminine self-gratification; those tapering fingers were the source of the bewildering muffler, for they held two bone needles and never ceased to move.

The volatile stitchery they produced occupied all the carpetless area of the floor and, in places, was piled up as high as the crippled knees of its maker. There was yards and yards of it in the room, perhaps even miles and miles of it, and I stepped through and across it very carefully, nudging it out of the way with my toes, to arrive where the girl directed me with her gun, in the position of a suppliant before the bathchair. The crippled being who lay in it had the most regal cast of chin and mouth imaginable and the proud, sad air of the king of a rainy country. One of her profiles was that of a beautiful woman, the other that of a beautiful man. It is a defect in our language there is no term of reference for these indeterminate and undefinable beings; but, although she acknowledged no gender, I will call her "she" because she had put on a female garment, a loose negligé of spider-colored lace, unless she, like the spiders, spun and wove her own thread and so had become clothed, for her shadowy hair was also the color of the stuff she knitted and so evanescent in texture it seemed to move of its own accord on the air around her. Her eyelids and the cavernous sockets of her eyes were thickly stuck with silver sequins that glittered in the strange, subaqueous, drowned, drowning light that suffused the room, a light filtered through windows caked with grime and half covered by creeper, clairvoyant light reflected, with an enhanced strangeness, by the immense mirror in a chipped gilt frame hanging on the wall opposite the fireplace; it seemed the mirror, like the moon, was itself endowed with the light it gave back to us.

With a touching fidelity, the mirror duplicated the room and all it contained, the fireplace, the walls covered with a stained white paper stippled with fronds of greenery, every piece of neglected ormolu furniture. How pleased I was to see my experiences had not changed me! though my old tweed suit was stained with grass, my stick gone— left behind where I had dropped it in the wood. And so much dirt on my face. But I looked as if I were reflected in a forest pool rather than by silvered glass for the surface of the mirror looked like the surface of motionless water, or of mercury, as though it were a solid mass of liquid kept in place by some inversion of gravity that reminded me of the ghastly weight of the shell that now dropped at the androgyne's feet from the dog's mouth. She never stopped knitting for one moment as she nudged it with a beautiful toe painted with a rime of silver; woe gave her a purely female face.

"Only one little stitch! And I only dropped one little stitch!" she mourned. And she bowed her head over her work in an ecstasy of regret.

"At least it wasn't out long," said the girl. Her voice

had a clanging resonance; mercy was a minor key that would never modify its martial music. "*He* found it!"

She gestured towards me with her gun. The androgyne directed upon me a pair of vague, too-large, stagnant eyes that did not shine.

"Do you know where this shell comes from?" she asked me with a grave courtesy.

I shook my head.

"It comes from the Sea of Fertility. Do you know where *that* is?"

"On the surface of the moon," I answered. My voice sounded coarse and rough to me.

"Ah," she said, "the moon, the source of polarized light. Yes and no to your reply. It is an equivalence. The sea of fertility is a reversed system, since everything there is as dead as this shell."

"He found it in the wood," said the girl.

"Put it back where it belongs, Anna," said the androgyne, who possessed a frail yet absolute air of authority. "Before any harm is done."

The girl bent and picked up the shell. She scrutinized the mirror and took aim at some spot within it that seemed to her a logical target for the shell. I saw her raise her arm to throw the shell into the mirror and I saw her mirrored arm raise the shell to throw it outside the mirror. Then she threw the duplicated shell. There was no sound in the room but the click of the knitting needles when she threw the shell into the mirror while her reflection threw the shell out of the mirror. The shell, when it met its own reflection, disappeared immediately.

The androgyne sighed with satisfaction.

"The name of my niece is Anna," she said to me, "because she can go both ways. As, indeed, I can myself, though I am not a simple palindrome."

She gave me an enigmatic smile and moved her shoulders so that the lace negligé she wore fell back from her soft, pale breasts that were, each one, tipped with nipples of deep, dark pink, with the whorled crenellations of raspberries, and then she shifted her loins a little to display, savage and barbaric in their rude, red-purple repose, the phallic insignia of maleness.

"She can," said Anna, "go both ways, although she cannot move at all. So her power is an exact equivalent of her impotence, since both are absolute."

But her aunt looked down at her soft weapon and said gently: "Not, my darling, *absolutely* absolute. Potency, impotence *in potentia,* hence relative. Only the intermediary, since indeterminate."

With that, she caressed her naked breasts with a stunted gesture of her forearms; she could not move her arms freely because she did not stop knitting. They looked at one another and laughed. Their laughter drove icicles of fear into my brain and I did not know which way to turn.

"You see, we must do away with you," said the androgyne. "You know too much."

Panic broke over me like a wave. I plunged across the room towards the door, careless of Anna's gun in my attempted flight. But my feet were snared by the knitting and once again I plunged downwards but this time my fall half stunned me. I lay dazed while their renewed laughter darted cruelly about the room.

"Oh," said Anna, "but we shan't kill you. We shall send you through the mirror. We shall send you where the shell went, since that is where you belong, now."

"But the shell vanished," I said.

"No," replied the androgyne. "It did not vanish in reality. That shell had no business in this world. I dropped a stitch, this morning; only one little stitch . . . and that confounded shell slipped through the hole the dropped stitch made, because those shells are all so very, very heavy, you see. When it met its reflection, it returned to its proper place. It cannot come back, now; and neither will you, after we have sent you through the mirror."

Her voice was so very gentle, yet she offered me a perpetual estrangement. I let out a cry. Anna turned to her aunt and placed her hand on her genitalia, so that the cock sprang up. It was of redoubtable size.

"Oh, auntie, don't scare him!" she said.

Then they tittered, the weird harpies, so that I was quite beside myself with fear and bewilderment.

"It is a system of equivalences," said the androgyne. "She carries the gun, you see; and I, too."

She displayed her towering erection with the air of a demonstrator in a laboratory.

"In my intermediary and cohesive logic, the equivalences reside beyond symbolism. The gun and the phallus are similar in their connection with life—that is, one gives it; and the other takes it away, so that both, in essence, are similar in that the negation freshly states the affirmed proposition."

I was more bewildered than ever.

"But do all the men in the mirror world have guns between their thighs?"

Anna exclaimed with irritation at my simplicity.

"That's no more likely than that I could impregnate you with this—" she said, pointing her gun at me, "here or in any other world."

"Embrace yourself in the mirror," said the androgyne, knitting, knitting, knitting away. "You must go, now. Now!"

Anna maintained her menace; there was nothing for it but to do as they bid. I went to the mirror and examined myself in its depths. A faint ripple ran over its surface; but when I touched it with my fingers, the surface was just as smooth and hard as it should have been. I saw that my reflection was cut off at the thighs by the gilt frame and Anna said: "Climb on a stool! Who'd want you truncated, here or there?"

She grinned in an appalling fashion and slipped back the safety catch on her rifle. So I pulled a little, cane-seated, gilt-backed chair to the mirror and clambered up. I gazed at myself in the mirror; there I was, complete from head to toe, and there they were, behind me, the androgyne weaving her ethereal coils and the armed young girl, who, now that she could kill me with one little flick of her finger, looked as beautiful as a Roman soldier plundering a North African city, with her rapist's eyes and her perfume of murder.

"Kiss yourself," commanded the androgyne in a swooning voice. "Kiss yourself in the mirror, the symbolic matrix of this and that, hither and thither, outside and inside."

Then I saw, even if I could no longer be astonished, that though she knitted in both the room and the mirror, there was, within the room, no ball of wool at all; her yarn emanated from inside the mirror and the ball of wool existed only in the medium of reflection. But I did not have time to wonder at this marvel for the rank stench of Anna's excitement filled the room and her hand trembled. Out of rage and desperation, I advanced my own lips to meet the familiar yet unknown lips that advanced towards mine in the silent world of the glass.

I thought these lips would be cold and lifeless; that I would touch them but they could not touch me. Yet, when the twinned lips met, they cleaved, for these mirrored lips of mine were warm and throbbed. This mouth was wet and contained a tongue, and teeth. It was too much for me. The profound sensuality of this unexpected caress crisped the roots of my sex and my eyes involuntarily closed while my arms clasped my own tweed shoulders. The pleasure of the embrace was intense; I swooned beneath it.

When my eyes opened, I had become my own reflection. I had passed through the mirror and now I stood on a little, cane-seated, gilt-backed chair with my mouth pressed to an impervious surface of glass I had misted with my own breath and moistened with my own saliva.

Anna cried: "Hurrah!" She dropped her rifle and clapped her hands while her aunt, continuing, all the time, to knit, gave me a peculiarly sultry smile.

"So," she said. "Welcome. This room is the halfway house between here and there, between this and that, because, you understand, I am so ambiguous. Stay in the field of force of the mirror for a while, until you are used to everything."

The first thing that struck me was, the light was black. My eyes took a little time to grow accustomed to this absolute darkness for, though the delicate apparatus of cornea and aqueous humor and crystalline lens and vitreous body and optic nerve and retina had all been reversed when I gave birth to my mirror self through the mediation of the looking-glass, yet my sensibility remained as it had been. So at first, through the glass, I saw darkly and all was confusion but for their faces, which were irradiated by familiarity. But, when the inside of my head could process the information my topsy-turvy senses retrieved for me, then my other or anti-eyes apprehended a world of phosphorescent color etched as with needles of variegated fire on a dimensionless opacity. The world was the same; yet absolutely altered. How can I describe it . . . almost as if this room was the color negative of the other room. Unless—for how could I ever be certain which was the primary world and which the secondary—the other room, the other house, the other wood that I saw, transposed yet still peeping through the window in the other mirror—all that had been the color negative of the room in which I now stood, where the exhalations of my breath were the same as the inhalations of my mirror-anti-twin who turned away from me as I turned away from him, into the distorted, or else really real, world of the mirror room, which, since it existed in this mirror in this room beyond the mirror, reflected all of this room's ambiguities and was no longer the room I had left. That endless muffler or web wound round the room, still, but now it wound round contrariwise and Anna's aunt was knitting from left to right, instead of from right to left, with hands, I realized, had they wished, could have pulled a right-hand glove over the left hand and vice versa, since she was truly ambidextrous.

But when I looked at Anna, I saw she was exactly the same as she had been on the other side of the mirror and knew her face for one of those rare faces that possess an absolute symmetry, each feature the exact equivalent of the other, so one of her profiles could serve as the template for both. Her skull was like a proposition in geometry. Irreducible as stone, finite as a syllogism, she was always indistinguishable from herself whichever way she went.

But the imperturbably knitting androgyne had turned its face contrariwise. One half of its face was always masculine and the other, no matter what, was feminine; yet these had been changed about, so that all the balances of the planes of the face and the lines of the brow were the opposite of what they had been before, although one half of the face was still feminine and the other masculine. Nevertheless, the quality of the difference made it seem that this altered yet similar face was the combination of the reflection of the female side of the face and the masculine side of the face that *did not appear* in the face I had seen beyond the mirror; the effect was as of the reflection of a reflection, like an example of perpetual regression, the perfect, self-sufficient nirvana of the hermaphrodite. She was Tiresias, capable of prophetic projection, whichever side of the mirror she chose to offer herself to my sight upon; and she went on knitting and knitting and knitting, with an infernal suburban complacency.

When I turned from the mirror, Anna was holding out her right or left hand towards me but, although I felt sure I was walking towards her and lifted up my legs and set them down again with the utmost determination, Anna receded further and further away from me. Niece and aunt emitted a titter and I guessed that, in order to come to Anna, I must go away from her. Therefore I stepped sturdily backwards and, in less than a second, her hard, thin, sunburned hand grasped mine.

The touch of her hand filled me with a wild loneliness.

With her other hand, she opened the door. I was terribly afraid of that door, for the room that contained the mirror was all that I knew, and therefore my only safety, in this unknown world that Anna, who now smiled inscrutably at me, negotiated as skillfully as if she herself, the solstice in person, went on curious hinges between this place and that place unlike her aunt, who, since she was crippled, could not move unless her condition of permanent stasis meant she was moving too fast for me to see, with a speed the inertia of the eye registered as immobility.

But, when the door creaked open on everyday, iron hinges that had never been oiled in this world or any other world, I saw only the staircase up which Anna had led me, down which she would now lead me, and the muffler that still curled down to the hall. The air was dank, just as it had been. Only, all the alignments of the stairwell had been subtly altered and the light was composed of a reversed spectrum.

The webs of the spiders presented structures of white fire so minutely altered from those I had passed on my way upstairs that only memory made me apprehend how their geometrical engineering had all been executed backwards. So we passed under the spectral arch they had prepared for us and out into the open air that did not refresh my bewildered brain, for it was as solid as water, dense and compact, of an impermeable substance that transmitted neither sound nor odor. To move through this liquid silence demanded the utmost exertion of physical energy and intellectual concentration, for gravity, beyond the mirror, was not a property of the ground but of the atmosphere. Then Anna, who understood the physical laws of this world, exerted a negative pressure upon me by some willed absence of impulse and to my amazement I now moved as if propelled sharply from behind along the path to the gate, past flowers that distilled inexpressible colors from the black sky above us, colors whose names only exist in an inverted language you could never understand if I were to speak it. But the colors were virtually independent of the forms of the plants. Haloes of incandescence, they had arbitrarily settled about spread umbrellas of petals as thin yet as hard as the shoulder blade of a rabbit, for the flesh of the flowers was calcified and lifeless; no plant was sentient in this coral garden. All had suffered a dead sea change.

And the black sky possessed no dimension of distance, nor gave none; it did not arch above us but looked as if it were pasted behind the flat outlines of the half-ruinous house that now lay behind us, a shipwreck bearing a marvelous freight, the female man or virile woman clicking away at her needles in a visible silence. A visible silence, yes; for the dense fluidity of the atmosphere did not transmit sound to me as sound, but, instead, as irregular kinetic abstractions etched upon its interior, so that, once in the new wood, a sinister, mineral, realm of undiminishable darkness, to listen to the blackbird was to watch a moving point inside a block of deliquescent glass. I saw these sounds because my eyes took in a different light than the light that shone on my breast when my heart beat on the other side of it, although the wood through whose now lateral gravity Anna negotiated me was the same wood in which I had been walking when I first heard her sing.

And I cannot tell you, since there is no language in this world to do so, how strange the antithetical wood and sweet June day were, for both had become the systematic negation of its others.

Anna, in some reversed fashion, must still have been menacing me with her gun, since it was her impulse that moved me; on we went, just as we had come—but Anna, now, went before me, with the muzzle of her gun pressed in the belly of nothingness, and the dog, her familiar, this time in the van. And this dog was white as snow and its balls were gone; on this side of the mirror, all dogs were bitches and vice versa.

I saw wild garlic and ground elder and the buttercups and daisies in the fossilized undergrowth now rendered in vivacious yet unnamable colors, as immobile arabesques without depth. But the sweetness of the wild roses rang in my ears like a peal of windbells for the vibrations of the perfumes echoed on my eardrums like the pulse of my own blood since, though they had become a kind of sound, they could not carry in the same way that sound did. I could not, for the life of me, make up my mind which world was which for I understood this world was coexistent in time and space with the other wood—was, as it were, the polarization of that other wood, although it was in no way similar to the reflection the other wood, or this wood, might have made in a mirror.

The more my eyes grew accustomed to the dark, the less in common did the petrified flora seem to have with anything I knew. I perceived all had been starkly invaded with, yes, shells, enormous shells, giant and uninhabited shells, so we might have been walking in the ruins of a marine city; the cool, pale coloring of those huge shells now glowed with a ghostly otherness and they were piled and heaped upon one another to parody the landscape of the woodland, unless the trees parodied them; all were whorled the wrong way round, all had that deathly weight, the supernatural resonance of the shell which seduced me and Anna told me in a soundless language I understood immediately that the transfigured wood, fertile now, only of metamorphoses, was—for how could it be anything else—the Sea of Fertility. The odor of her violence deafened me.

Then, once again, she began to sing; I saw the mute, dark, fire burning like Valhalla in *Götterdämmerung*. She sang a funeral pyre, the swan's song, death itself, and, with a brusque motion of her gun, she forced me forward on my knees while the dog stood over me as she tore open my clothes. The serenade smoldered all around us and I was so much at the mercy of the weight of the air, which pressed down on me like a coffin lid, and of the viscosity of the atmosphere, that I could do nothing to defend myself, even if I had known how, and soon she had me, poor, forked thing, stretched out upon a bank of shells with my trousers around my knees. She smiled but I could not tell what the smile meant; on this side of the mirror, a smile was no clue whatsoever to intention or to feeling and I did not think she meant to do me a good deed as she unbuckled her uncouth leather belt and stepped out of her jeans.

Parting the air with the knives of her arms, she precipitated herself upon me like a quoit on a peg. I screamed; the notes of my scream rose up on the air like Ping-Pong balls on a jet of water at a fun-fair. She raped me; perhaps her gun, in this system, gave her the power to do so.

I shouted and swore but the shell grotto in which she ravished me did not reverberate and I only emitted gobs of light. Her rape, her violation of me, caused me atrocious physical and mental pain. My being leaked away from me under the visitation of her aggressive flesh. My self grew less in agony under the piston thrust of her slender loins, as if she were a hammer and were forging me into some other substance than flesh and spirit. I knew the dreadful pleasure of abandonment; she had lit my funeral pyre and now would kill me. I felt such outrage I beat in the air behind my head with my helpless fists as she pumped away indefatigably at my sex, and to my surprise, I saw her face cloud and bruises appear on it, although my hands were nowhere near her. She was a brave girl; she only fucked the harder, for she was intransigent and now resembled the Seljuk Turks sacking Constantinople. I knew there was no hope for me if I did not act immediately.

Her gun lay propped against the shells beside us. I reached the other way and seized it. I shot at the black sky while she straddled me. The bullet pierced a neat, round, empty hole in the flat vault of the heavens but no light, no sound, leaked through; I had made a hole without quality but Anna let out a ripping shriek that sent a jagged scar across the surface of the wood. She tumbled backwards and twitched a little. The dog growled at me, a terrible sight, and leaped at my throat but I quickly shot her, also, in this negative way and, now free, there remained only the problem of the return to the mirror, the return to the right-hand side of the world. But I kept tight hold of the gun, by grasping it loosely, because of the guardian of the mirror.

To return to the house, I struck out from the shell grotto

where Anna lay, in the opposite direction from the one we had come from. I must have fallen into a mirror elision of reflected time, or else I stumbled upon a physical law I could not have guessed at, for the wood dissolved, as if the blood that leaked from Anna's groin was a solvent for its petrified substance, and now I found myself back at the crumbling gate before her juices were dry on my cock. I paused to do up my fly before I made my way to the door; I used my arms like scissors to snip through the thickness of the atmosphere, for it grew, moment by moment, less liquid and more impalpable. I did not ring the bell, so great was my outrage, so vivid my sense of having been the plaything of these mythic and monstrous beings.

The knitting curled down the stairs, just as I expected, and, in another moment, I saw, on a staccato stave, the sound of the needles.

She, he, it, Tiresias, though she knitted on remorselessly, was keening over a whole dropped row of stitches, trying to repair the damage as best she could. Her keening filled the room with a Walpurgisnacht of crazy shapes and, when she saw I was alone, she flung back her head and howled. In that decompression chamber between here and there, I heard a voice as clear as crystal describe a wordless song of accusation.

"Oh, my Anna, what have you done with my Anna—?"

"I shot her," I cried. "With her own weapon."

"A rape! She's raped!" screamed the androgyne as I dragged the gilt chair to the mirror and clambered upon it. In the silvered depths before me, I saw the new face of a murderer I had put on behind the mirror.

The androgyne, still knitting, kicked with her bare heels

upon the floor to drive her bathchair over the wreathing muffler towards me, in order to attack me. The bathchair cannoned into the chair on which I stood and she rose up in it as far as she could and began to beat me with her tender fists. But, because she did not stop knitting, she offered no resistance when I brought my ham-hand crashing down on her working face. I broke her nose; bright blood sprang out. I turned to the mirror as she screamed and dropped her knitting.

She dropped her knitting as I crashed through the glass
    through the glass, glass splintered round me driving unmercifully into my face
        through the glass, glass splintered
          through the glass—
            half through.

Then the glass gathered itself together like a skillful whore and expelled me. The glass rejected me; it sealed itself again into nothing but mysterious, reflective opacity. It became a mirror and it was impregnable.

Balked, I stumbled back. In Tiresias's bed-sitting room, there was the most profound silence, and nothing moved; the flow of time might have stopped. Tiresias held her empty hands to her face that was now irretrievably changed; each one snapped clean in two, her knitting needles lay on the floor. Then she sobbed and flung out her arms in a wild, helpless gesture. Blood and tears splashed down on her robe, but in a baleful, hopeless way she began to laugh, although time must have started again and now moved with such destructive speed that, before my eyes, that ageless being withered—a quick frost touched her. Wrinkles sprang out on her pale forehead while her hair fell from her head in great armfuls and her negligé turned brown and crumbled away, to reveal all the flesh that sagged from the bone as I watched it. She was the ruins of time. She grasped her throat and choked. Perhaps she was dying. The muffler was blowing away like dead leaves in a wind that sprang up from nowhere and raced through the room, although the windows stayed shut tight. But Tiresias spoke to me; she spoke to me once again.

"The umbilical cord is cut," she said. "The thread is broken. Did you not realize who I was? That I was the synthesis in person? For I could go any way the world goes and so I was knitting the thesis and the antithesis together, this world and that world. Over the leaves and under the leaves. Cohesion gone. Ah!"

Down she tumbled, the bald old crone, upon a pile of wisps of unraveled grey wool as the ormolu furniture split apart and the paper unfurled from the wall. But I was arrogant; I was undefeated. Had I not killed her? Proud as a man, I once again advanced to meet my image in the mirror. Full of self-confidence, I held out my hands to embrace my self, my anti-self, my self not-self, my assassin, my death, the world's death.

Elegy for a Freelance

I REMEMBER YOU as clearly as if you'd died yesterday, though I don't remember you often—usually, I'm far too busy. But I told the commissar about you, once. I asked him if I'd done the right thing; would he have done the same? But he said, if I wanted absolution, that he was the last person to ask for it, and, besides, everything is changed, now, and we are not the same.

I remember that I was living high up in an attic, in a house in a square. Most of the windows in the other houses round the square were boarded up and planks were nailed across the doors but they were not uninhabited. Although all these houses were waiting to be pulled down, they contained a handful of small, scarcely licit households whose members crept in and out through secret entries, lived by candlelight, slept upon the filthy mattresses the dossers who lived there before them had used and ate stews made from vegetables picked out of the greengrocers' garbage cans and butchers' bones begged for dogs that did not exist.

But our landlord—it was legal to own private property, to rent it out, in those days—refused to sell his house to the speculators who wanted to pull the entire terrace down. He'd spent the blitz in his house; it was his foxhole. He pulled the carious walls up snug around his ears and felt himself enveloped in a safety that, although it was fictive, he believed in completely. He rented his rooms out at old-fashioned rents because he did not know that times had changed; how could he? He never left home. He was confined to a chair and almost blind. His room was his world, his house the unknown universe he knew of but never ventured into. Everything else was unknowable. He did not even know that the boys who lived in the basement filled milk bottles with gasoline in their back room and made explosions.

A girl lived with them in the basement. She was fifteen. Her face was pale, mild and plump and always seemed a little surprised that she found herself stumbling under the weight of a pregnancy that had stunned her. She hardly ever spoke and moved with the heaviness of somebody moving underwater. You kept a rifle in our room and loved to sit and scan the square and the street below us from the open window.

A young man and a girl came to do yoga in the square every morning. They adopted the tree position. A child on the swings swung more and more idly; he twisted round to watch them. They always had the same audience, the children in the playground and the apprentice sniper. They unfurled their right legs from the hip and reefed them in at the knee in order to place the soles of their bare right feet against the inner sides of their upper left thighs. They joined their hands together as if in prayer and then raised their joined hands above their heads. In order to keep their balance, they fixed their eyes on the worn grass in front of them with the utmost concentration. They maintained this position for an entire minute—I watched the hand on my watch move—and then they returned their right feet to the ground as they lowered their hands and arms and now raised their left legs in order to repeat the exercise. When it was over, they decorously stood on their heads. They were rapt with devotion.

X watched them through the sights of his rifle while they went through the entire repertory of movements. I was scared out of my wits when he slipped back the safety catch and did not dare say anything. I knew the couple below by sight. They squatted in a house on the other side of the square. They were harmless as the pigeons who lived on the roof. When they had finished, they went away again. X replaced the safety catch and laughed. I was very frightened of him in his feral moods but he told me an authentic assassin ought to be as indifferent as the weather and, when he scanned the square, all he was doing was practicing indifference.

I went into his world when I fell in love with him and felt only a sense of privilege in its isolation. We had purposely exiled ourselves from the course of everyday events and were proud to live in parentheses. I went out for a little air at night, sometimes, when the streets were flooded with the ghastly yellow light that bleaches the blood that runs out of road accidents so that it doesn't look real. I used to walk through the streets for miles and I would clap my hands with childlike pleasure, I would enthusiastically applaud the detonating termini.

It hardly seemed possible the city could survive that summer. The sky opened like the clockwork Easter eggs the Tsars gave one another. The night would part, like two halves of a dark shell, and spill explosions. Because I lived in a house full of amateur terrorists, I felt I myself lit the fuses and caused these displays of pyrotechnics. Then I would feel almost omnipotent, just as X did, when he sat with his rifle above the square at the window of my room.

I was living high up in an attic. I hung over the summer in my attic as though it were the gondola of a balloon. London lay below me with her legs wide open; she was a whore sufficiently accommodating to find room for us in her embraces, even though she cost so much to love.

She is so old she ought to be superannuated, you said, the old cow. She paints so thickly over the stratified residue of yesterday and the day before yesterday and the day before the day before's cosmetics you can hardly make out the wens and blemishes under all the layers of paint, graffiti and old posters—voluptuous, oppressive, corrupt, self-regarding London marinating in the syrup of her own decay like baba au rhum, while the property speculators burrow away at her guts with the vile diligence of gonococci.

A feverish, hysterical glamour played over this wasting city like summer lightning. While I watched it, the city changed shape. Towers of steel and glass thrust their way through the soft, soiled velvet rind of the rotting fruit.

Nobody lived in those towers; how could anybody live there—like the architecture of the Third Reich, they looked as if they were intended to be most beautiful in ruins. Among this architecture of desolation, haunting the rat-infested rubble, mendicants and proselytizers rang bells and rattled tambourines as they offered to the passerby a bewildering variety of salvations. Those in saffron robes who had shaved their heads invoked the gods of the Indian subcontinent though our neighbors told us we ought to trust in Jesus. But *our* salvation would be gelignite; the basement of the house in which I lived had become a little arsenal. Any wise child can get a hand grenade together; it was the time of the Children's Crusade.

It was a strange, suspended time. The city had never looked more beautiful but I did not know, then, that it seemed to me beautiful only because it was doomed and I was the innocent slave of bourgeois aesthetics, that always sees an elegiac charm in decay. I remember velvet nights spiked with menace and the beautiful showers of sparks when an amateur incendiarist ignited a police station. My house was always full of the shimmering sound of the trees in the square moving in the wind, so that it seemed the sea was rushing through the corridors, the rooms.

I was living on the fourth floor although I had such vertigo that the sight of any abyss, however insignificant, excited in me, almost intolerably, the desire to plunge. I was quite helpless before the attraction of gravity. I was overwhelmed. I became powerless. Therefore to live on the fourth floor meant that every day began with a small triumph of will over instinct. I wanted to jump; but I must not jump. Pallor, shallow breathing, a prickle of cold sweat—I exhibited all the symptoms of panic, as I did when

I met X. *That* was like finding myself on the edge of an abyss but the vertigo that I felt then came from a sense of recognition. This abyss was that of my own emptiness; I plunged instantly, for my innocence was so perfect that I saw in this submission the height of sophistication.

It was as lovely a summer as those that precede wars. The West Indian lady who ran the neighborhood launderette always wore a small felt hat with a veil, as if she were determined to keep up appearances even in the most extreme circumstances. She pushed the dirt around the floor with a sodden mop and, when her tasks were finished, she would sit on a chair and read her well-thumbed Bible aloud to herself in that ineffable, querulous lilt, like the voice of a reproachful bird. Sometimes she would exclaim over the things she found in the book; when I looked over her shoulder, once, while she was crying: HOSANNA! I saw she was reading the Apocalypse.

The squatters consecrated the house next door. All night long, while we fixed up our explosive devices in the basement, they chanted: BABY JESUS, BABY JESUS, BABY JESUS.

I would not have believed Lenin was right when he said there was no place for orgy in the revolution, even if I had read Lenin then. What we were about in bed seemed to be activity that could in itself overturn the world. X's lycanthropic eyes glowed in the dark like fuses. I found most pleasure of all in the delicious dread that seized me when he clung too close. I wanted to be the Madonna of the Barricades; I would have shot anybody you told me to but only if they did not get hurt. I felt I needed to understand nothing beyond my own sensations. I felt, as primitives do, that ceremonials such as the ones we made could revivify dead earth. Your kisses along my arms were like tracer bullets. I am lost. I flow. Your flesh defines me. I become your creation. I am your fleshly reflection.

("Libido and false consciousness characterized sexual relations during the last crisis of capital," says the commissar.)

A man constructs his own fate out of his sense of the world. You engaged in conspiracies because you believed the humblest objects were engaged in a conspiracy against you. Your conviction was contagious; it impressed me. "Even the strawberries smell of blood, this summer," you remarked with anticipatory relish. I found you more and more often at the window, practicing indifference.

You described the state of permanent revolution to me. It sounded like a series of beautiful explosions. Volcano after volcano would erupt under their own internal stresses in an endless reduplication of ecstasy. When the bed creaked beneath us, it sounded like the *liebestod* from *Tristan and Isolde* performed with vehemence by a military band. The grand design of glorious convulsions you depicted was so beautiful I wept; but we would begin, you said, in small ways, we would begin with a single shooting. You made assassination sound as enticing as pornography. A, B, and C were suspicious of me since you abandoned the basement for my bed. Now we were all gripped in the same obsession, they treated me more politely. *Folie à deux, à trois, à quatre.* We were living on the crater of a volcano and felt the earth move beneath us. What stirring times! What seismographic times!

("The bourgeoisie turned politics into an aspect of romanticism," says the commissar. "If it was only an art form, how could it threaten them?")

The city unraveled like knitting as the transport workers'

strikes imposed vast distances between its various sections but we never went beyond walking distance of our house so the strikes did not affect us.

Our house was tall and narrow. Worn steps led down to the area. Our landlord lived in the front room on the ground floor. He crouched in front of his television set making what sense he could out of the random flickering that was all his eyes registered, poor old thing, with his stick and his cats. He had a sink and a gas ring and a little cupboard where he kept his cats' fish. He boiled up their dinners twice a week and stored their food in a plastic washing-up bowl when it was cooked. The house stank of stale fish; we had to burn incense all the time to cancel out the smell. He spread his table with clean newspapers and set out the fish for his cats in separate saucers. They all jumped up to eat. There was a soup plate full of water which, although it was refreshed each day, always managed to drown a fly or two by lunchtime, and a saucer of milk that had turned into junket by the six o'clock news. His three-legged chairs were balanced on piles of old newspapers and upholstered with cast-off garments. Cats of all colors sat upon the sideboard among the empty brown ale bottles, the open cans of condensed milk, the stopped clock, the yellowing circulars, the football coupons, the curded milk bottles, the plaster Alsatian dog with one ear chipped. There he sat, a king in his kingdom, thumping upon the floor when the conspirators in the basement went *bang!* by accident.

Once a week, in turn, we visited him to pay our rents for we were determined to be scrupulous and, if you must have a landlord at all, it's best if he's purblind. It was like paying tribute to a holy statue. Age had drawn his yellow, freckled skin so tight across his skull his head shone like polished bone and his eyes had faded to the innocent blue of baby ribbon—wandering, rheumy eyes, gummed at the corners. His bony fingers clutched the handle of his stick with a certain balked ferocity.

He was afraid of us, I suppose, and so he pretended to be fierce. In the pub, they said he kept roll upon roll of banknotes stored in Old Holborn tins tucked away here and there among the clutter. He ingested his rents like a sponge but he suspected nothing although the cats did and threshed their tails when we went into his room. Sometimes they spat. The ginger one once scratched you.

A middle-aged transvestite lived on the first floor but he was too immersed in his aberration to pay us much attention. He ventured out for little walks around the square in the dusk that tenderly veiled his eccentricity, tottering on his five-inch heels, spiking the ground before him in the manner of a climber with the point of his long, furled umbrella. He wore a black gabardine two-piece with a pencil skirt for these expeditions and slung a fox fur round his neck. The mask hung over his left shoulder and kept a good lookout behind with its little, beady eyes. Above him, a slack-witted unmarried mother pigged it with her brood. She did the old man's shopping for him, when she remembered, but he only wanted the fish, twice a week, a can or two of beans and the occasional bottle of brown ale.

A perpetual twilight dominated that house, with its characteristic odors of stale cooking, phantom bacon, lavatories and the cats who pissed in the hall. The bulbs on the stairways were always blown. It was an old, dark house; it was a cave. We saw visions on the walls. It was a slum.

It was a citadel. That was the time of the freelance assassins; our cell was self-sufficient and took no orders nor cognizance of any other cell in the cancerous growth of the deathwardly inclining city. You had the plausibility of a Nechaev; to plot a murder became your sole preoccupation.

You arbitrarily selected a member of the cabinet. We consulted the I Ching, we threw the coins. The oracle seemed to be propitious, although, as always, its tone was guarded. We drew lots. Inexorably, the marked card found you. In the full consciousness of a young man about to become an assassin, you made love to me like the storming of the Bastille. But then I found you'd somewhere encountered an obstacle to indifference for now you were crying, though, when I asked why you were crying, you hit me.

Our neighbors were chanting so loudly they might have been chanting in the same room and I had no curtains at the window so the glaring, yellow light balefully illuminated your unhappy face, but I was too much under your spell to guess why you were crying. Hadn't everything been decided? Tomorrow we would go and murder the politician. I would ring the doorbell and then you would fire the gun. I could not understand why you were crying, you had so successfully impressed me with the model simplicity of the plan, so that I was sure we were in the right. I went to sleep again, sulking because I had been hit. The monotonous, droning chant—BABY JESUS, BABY JESUS, BABY JESUS—lulled me to sleep.

What an awakening!—there was so much blood on your shirt. You spilled the banknotes over me. They were in tight little blue rolls that bounced off my body, unfurling as they fell to the floor. Such a lot of money! I blinked in the violet dawn, astounded at the extravagance of your hysteria. You sobbed and babbled and hurled the furniture to the ground, smashed cups, overturned the wastepaper basket. I made you tea and slyly stoked up the mug with sleeping pills. I choked it down you and got you into the bed I had vacated for I could never lie in the same bed with you, now. I stayed with you until I was certain you were sleeping and locked the door behind you.

A, B and C had finished the night's work and were frying eggs and bread on their gas ring. A's girl lay on the mattress under her belly which was the size and shape of a dirigible, round enough, big enough to rise up into the air and carry her away with it from this vale of tears, over the rainbow, to a happy land far, far away. I told them what you had said to me, that you killed him for practice. We had intended to be such philosophic assassins! But what were your existential credentials when you murdered the landlord? Was it the dress rehearsal for an assassination or the audition of an assassin?

The old man lay on the floor in his rank pajamas. His debilitated, senescent tool dangled out of his yellowed fly. The cats milled about him, mewing ravenously. There was blood on their whiskers and on their inquisitive paws. X had smashed in the old man's skull and he'd tumbled off the bed in his death agony. In spite of his age and weakness, he had put up a struggle; we could see the signs of it all over the room. The bedclothes were disordered and his little night table had been knocked over. The chamber pot it contained had fallen out on its side, spilling its contents on the floor. Then X must have gone through every cupboard and drawer in the room to find the fabled tobacco tins of money. We looked at the evidence in silence though all the time the neighbors went on wailing very loudly. We could hear them downstairs, even here, on the ground floor. The cats pressed against us, yowling, and I thought I had better feed the cats because I did not want them to practice necrophagy upon the landlord. I opened the food cupboard and took out their fish. I spread the table and laid out their meal as if nothing had happened. They all jumped up and tucked in, purring as they swallowed their dinners.

We had not let A's girl into the room because of her condition. Now, from behind the lace curtain, we saw her, with her shawl flung carelessly around her shoulders, pursuing her burden as it stumbled away down the street. A said: "She's broken—she's gone for the police." I rushed out of the house and ran after her. I soon caught up with her; she was too fat to run fast. She wept. She said how much she always disliked X; that he had cold eyes. Then she fainted. A came and helped me carry her back to the basement. Shortly after that, she went into labor. The neighbors continued to chant: BABY JESUS, BABY JESUS, BABY JESUS. While I held A's girl's frightened, hot, sticky hand and A heated water, B and C took some rope, went to my attic and tied X up. They said he was too surprised to struggle when they woke him. He must have felt it wa the revolt of the toys.

Then a police car drew up outside and we shrank into ourselves, we were so scared. Poor Susie moaned and tore at the mattress on which she lay. But the police had come for our neighbors. The transvestite had complained about the noise and we watched from the area steps as the police took an axe to the boards that were nailed over the front door and entered it. A little while later, they came out again, half-leading, half-carrying the dazed and shaking occupants, who were all as white as sheets, tranced, emaciated, their eyes staring as still they mumbled their orisons, too limp and listless to protest.

I sterilized my nail scissors in the gas jet and A held his wailing son in his arms after I cut the cord. But, however pleased A was to be a father, he insisted on a fair trial for X. Perhaps, even then, B and C didn't quite trust me; I'd been a rich girl. But X confessed everything to us all quite freely.

We tried him in the attic. We left Susie downstairs nursing her baby. We untied X's legs and let him sit down on a chair but we did not untie his arms. He confessed as follows; he seemed agonizingly torn between humiliation and self-justification.

"I wasn't sure, I wasn't sure of myself. I kept thinking, what if I blow it? If I'd blown the whole thing, hadn't been able to pull the trigger, had just stood there in the doorway staring vacantly at him. What if I can't kill when I want to kill and am in the right to kill? What if I were paralyzed? What if I'd spent so long looking at people through the sights of a rifle and holding back from shooting that I could never shoot? Fear I'd be weak shook me.

"What good did the landlord do to anyone? Sitting in his room, sucking in his rents. Nobody loves him. He's significant to nobody. He's hardly alive at all, he can't talk, hardly, he's almost blind, squatting like a toad on all that money.

"I was in a frenzy, I prayed. Yes, I did. The fear I'd fail threw me into a frenzy. I prayed and the answer came. I left her sleeping and took the gun and went to his room. He didn't wake up when I went in but the cats all woke and stretched themselves and jumped off the chairs and the sideboard and the bed and came towards me, mewing; it was a tide of fur with eyes and mouths in it. He woke up when he heard the cats and began to mew, too. 'Who's there, pussies, what's the matter, pussies?' I had nothing against him when I went into the room—nothing. It was only an exercise in self-control.

"But I began to hate him when I saw how helpless he was. When I saw how easy it would be to kill him, nothing to it, then I began to hate him. I raised the rifle and looked at him through the sights. The sights changed the way I saw him. Through the sights of the rifle, now I saw he was not human, not even an old wreck of humanity. He was only an object to be extinguished. He asked some menacing person he could not see if that person had come for his money. When I realized that person was I, I thought that I might just as well take his money, while I was here, since he offered it to me. But I said nothing and my hands were shaking. He told me not to kill him. That was how he reminded me I *could* kill him, if I wanted to. Up till then, I had not wanted to but when he called me his murderer, I became so. He sealed his own fate. It was his own fault, what happened.

"Next door they were chanting away like mad things. He rolled about on his filthy bed clutching his head with his hands as if his hands would protect it. His pajamas burst open and the old flesh spilled on the sheets. I felt nauseated to see his old flesh. My fingers tightened on the trigger. The cats screamed and pressed against my legs. The ginger one scratched me. They reared up on their hind legs and snarled, I could have sworn they were attacking me. How disgusting the old bedbug was, now he was at my mercy! But just as I was about to shoot, I thought: what a noise the gun will make. It will be much louder than the chanting, even. The noise will wake Sister Boy. Sister Boy will wake and throw his negligé round his shoulders and come and see what is the matter. The woman upstairs will wake, or her kids will wake. They'll all come down, even the four-year-old, wiping the sleep out of its eyes. I thought of a holocaust—mow them all down. But I was too self-restrained.

"I lowered the gun. He was fumbling in his little night table, where he keeps his pisspot. The night table rocked, he was fumbling so. Out jumped the pisspot and crashed on the ground. All the cats puffed out their fur, stuck up their backs and hissed and shrank away from me, because the crash of the pisspot startled them, but he was rummaging for his savings in the night table and found one little tin. He shook the banknotes all over the floor, they were rolled up in the tin like curling papers, they fell in the spilled piss and the cats pounced on them and began to pat them this way and that way with their paws. He scooped up some banknotes in his fists and shoved them towards me. He said: 'Take it, it's all I've got.' But I knew he had lots of other old tobacco tins full of money, doesn't everybody say so? When he tried to buy me off so cheaply, I lost all mercy and bludgeoned him about the head with the butt of the rifle until he stopped moving."

He looked at us as though he was certain we understood everything perfectly. I closed my eyes; I had the sensation of falling. Yet, when I opened my eyes, the abyss remained; I stood only upon its brink. Now my eyes were open, perception, lucidity became my new profession. At the conclusion of his story, X began to cry like a child, as though he were to be pitied, and then I felt most afraid of him, in case I began to pity him. While we watched him sniveling, we grew older. He cried like a baby and we became his parents. We must decide what would be best for him. Now I was his mother, they his father and we saw our common responsibility as his cause in the random nature of his effect.

"It must be worst for you," A said to me, because I'd been the lover of this person; but the same terror gripped us all, for our complicity with him was over once he had acted only for himself and by himself and now we could stand apart from him and, in judging him, judge ourselves.

I will try and describe you better. I am glad you died before the barricades went up. We served our time and took our punishment upon them but I would not have liked to have you beside me with a machine gun because you were your own hero, always your own hero, and would not have taken orders easily. But you might have made an exceptional Kamikaze pilot, had you not been so scared of dying. You made us believe you were our leader; so, while you were ordering us about, how could we become a confederacy? We were in the deepest complicity with you; we admired your paranoia. While we admired it, we believed it formed an explanation of events in itself. But I was always a little afraid of you because you clung to me far too tightly and made me come with the barbarous dexterity of a huntsman eviscerating a stag.

After we heard X's confession, we gave him some water to drink and tied him up again before we gagged him, in case he tried to cry to Sister Boy or the unmarried mother below for help. Then we went down to the basement to discuss what we should do with him. A's girl was suckling her baby. She seemed obscurely but entirely content with her own miracle. She was angry we had locked her into the basement and said she would never leave A because he was the father of her child but I thought she said that due to the emotion generated in the generation of the baby and we should still be wary of her. A cooked her some brown rice and vegetables and added a couple of eggs, because she needed nourishment. After a great deal of discussion, B took some food to X also, but X dashed the dish to the floor. He was petulant, now, B told us; he thought we were behaving irrationally.

He had quite recovered his old self-confidence, it seemed, but we no longer retained confidence in him. We reached our decision in unison, although C—what memories of old movies!—at first wanted to lock X alone in my attic with a revolver and let him take his own way out. But our consensus convinced C that X would not have done so, had we given him the chance.

B took a coil of stout rope from the cupboard under the sink. We waited until dark; we listened desultorily to the radio and heard the army had been called in to break the car workers' strike but we were all stricken with such dreadful gravity at the unexpected turn of events in our cell that the news did not move us. Our private situation seemed to us far more significant.

X was in a foul state since we had not untied him all day so now he rolled in his own excrement and stank. He was in a filthy temper and cursed us but, when he saw the rope, first he laughed to try to bluff his way out of the noose; and then he blubbered—there is no other word for his collapse in tears and pleadings. He seemed astonished we were capable of acting without him. A held the revolver. It wasn't far to Hampstead Heath.

We forced X along with his arms bound and the muzzle of the revolver in his back. We did not meet many others on the streets; those whom we did pass by edged away from us, they must have thought we were all drunk, and the Heath itself was empty apart from a distant bonfire that marked, probably, the camp of some homeless family. By now the moon was up; we soon found a suitable tree.

When X realized there was no hope for him, he relapsed into silence but, when I slipped the noose around his neck, he asked me if I loved him. I was surprised at that—it seemed to me so far from the point; but I replied, yes, I *had* loved him and I tested the running knot. B and C pulled the rope. Up he went, like a flag. There was a russet-colored moon of ominous size too low above the whispering bushes; he danced exuberantly for five minutes beneath it after the click when his neck broke. His bowels opened. What a mess!

When it hung limp, we cut his body down and threw it in the undergrowth. A vomited and B wept a little, but C and I covered it with leaves, like the robins in *Babes in the Wood.* I retained such a ferocious calm that C said to me, you are turning into a tiger lady when I always thought you were such a pussycat. I think that justice had been done, although we ourselves had been the perpetrators of both crime and punishment and we did not dig a hole to bury X because we wanted to leave a loophole in which the everyday circumstances of justice might catch up with us. We were beginning to behave with a certain dignity. Our illogic began to approach a kind of harsh virtue, although we looked at one another with veiled, estranged eyes; who were we, what were we becoming?

Was it possible we could have done what we had done; how could it have been possible we had planned what we had intended?

A's girl and the child slept quite peacefully in the basement where we made ourselves tea that did not taste any different from the tea we had drunk before we hanged him.

Now B revealed an intransigent morality. He wanted us to go to the police, make a clean breast of all and take our punishment, since we had done nothing of which we ourselves were ashamed. But A had his baby son to think of and wanted to take Susie and his child to a Welsh mountain where he had friends in a commune, there to recuperate from these excesses in the clean air. Apropos of nothing, he declared he'd never be able to look at meat again and would walk on the other side of the road when he passed a butcher's shop. He sat on the mattress by the sleeping girl and looked, every moment, more and more like an ordinary husband and father. But C and I did not know what to do, now, nor what to think. We felt nothing but a lapse of feeling, a dulled heaviness, a despair.

The pure, cool light of early September touched the contents of the room with fastidious fingers; we looked at the day with mild surprise, that it should be as bright as any other day, brighter, in fact, than most. Then I felt a drop like a heavy raindrop fall on the back of my hand but it was not a raindrop, for the sun was shining, nor a drop from a leaking cistern, because the landlord's room was directly over our heads. This was a red drop. Horror! It was blood; and, looking up, I saw the stain on the ceiling where the old man's blood was leaking through. Soon he would begin to smell.

We began to argue. Should we dig a hole in the backyard and bury the old man in it, pack our few things and leave the house under false names for secret destinations, as A wanted to do; or should we throw ourselves upon the law, as B thought was right. Instinct and will, again; I was poised on the window ledge of a fourth floor of a building I had never suspected existed and I did not know which was will and which was instinct that told me to jump, to run. While we were discussing these things, we heard a low rumble in the distance. We thought it was thunder but, when A turned on the radio to find out what time it was, only martial music was playing and the news flash informed us the coup had taken place; the army was in power, as if this was not home but a banana republic. They were encountering some resistance in the North but were rapidly crushing it. All the time we had been plotting, the generals had been plotting and we had known nothing. Nothing!

The thunder grew louder; it was gun and mortar fire. The sky soon filled with helicopters. The Civil War began. History began.

Afterword

I STARTED TO WRITE short pieces when I was living in a room too small to write a novel in. So the size of my room modified what I did inside it and it was the same with the pieces themselves. The limited trajectory of the short narrative concentrates its meaning. Sign and sense can fuse to an extent impossible to achieve among the multiplying ambiguities of an extended narrative. I found that, though the play of surfaces never ceased to fascinate me, I was not so much exploring them as making abstractions from them. I was writing, therefore, tales.

Though it took me a long time to realize why I liked them, I'd always been fond of Poe, and Hoffman—Gothic tales, cruel tales, tales of wonder, tales of terror, fabulous narratives that deal directly with the imagery of the unconscious—mirrors; the externalized self; forsaken castles;

haunted forests; forbidden sexual objects. Formally, the tale differs from the short story in that it makes few pretenses at the imitation of life. The tale does not log everyday experience, as the short story does; it interprets everyday experience through a system of imagery derived from subterranean areas behind everyday experience, and therefore the tale cannot betray its readers into a false knowledge of everyday experience.

The Gothic tradition in which Poe writes grandly ignores the value systems of our institutions; it deals entirely with the profane. Its great themes are incest and cannibalism. Character and events are exaggerated beyond reality, to become symbols, ideas, passions. Its style will tend to be ornate, unnatural—and thus operate against the perennial human desire to believe the word as fact. Its only humor is black humor. It retains a singular moral function—that of provoking unease.

The tale has relations with subliterary forms of pornography, ballad and dream, and it has not been dealt with kindly by literati. And is it any wonder? Let us keep the unconscious in a suitcase, as Père Ubu did with his conscience, and flush it down the lavatory when it gets too troublesome.

So I worked on tales. I was living in Japan; I came back to England in 1972. I found myself in a new country. It was like waking up, it was a rude awakening. We live in Gothic times. Now, to understand and to interpret is the main thing; but my method of investigation is changing.

These stories were written between 1970 and 1973 and are arranged in chronological order, as they were written. There is a small tribute to Defoe, father of the bourgeois novel in England, inserted in the story "Master."